I0727138

Ocean's Rise

DEMELZA CARLTON

Copyright © 2021 Demelza Carlton

Lost Plot Press

All rights reserved.

DEDICATION

For Pebbles, who learned too late the fate awaiting the cat who got the canary.

One

"Lass, I love you dearly, but I've scarcely slept in a fortnight, we've made love so late into the night. I know you rest during the day, but I can't sleep at work. What would the mine crews say? They'll be calling me Sleepy McGregor!"

I don't deny I was disappointed to have William's magnificent body lying beside instead of inside mine, but he told the truth: we'd made love more times than I could count since our stranding on West White Beach. It was as if we both knew our time together was constrained by the growth of the child inside me, for after her birth we'd be forever changed. We'd be a family.

Sighing, I snuggled against him and sank into sleep. No night-time swims for me any more – Mother patrolled the cove and the dolphins were everywhere, sharing gossip until it flowed faster than water. If I dipped a toe beneath the ocean's surface, she would hear of it. And William's life would be in danger.

It felt like I'd barely closed my eyes when William slipped out of bed, promising to see me at breakfast. Pregnancy made me more somnolent than ever – I nodded and went straight back to sleep, only to be woken by a kiss from William when the sun was high in the sky.

"You missed breakfast, lass, but if you hurry, you can be dressed in time to join me for lunch."

I scrambled out of bed and into suitable afternoon clothes, barely pausing to splash some water on my face before I reached for a comb to tame my sleep-tangled locks.

I'd managed to deal with half of it when I heard Sarah's quiet steps approaching. "How are you feeling this morning?" she asked.

I waited until she appeared in the doorway before I replied, "Fine. A little tired, is all." My stomach gurgled and my daughter kicked it from inside my womb. I wish I could see her angry face, for I was sure she would be. All the movement distracted me and I realised, "There's no morning sickness today!"

Sarah smiled. "It's about time it went away. You have the glow of motherhood about you now instead of the green tinge of illness."

Was my insatiable lust for William part of my pregnancy, or just my natural response to William's evident ardour for my increasingly rounded form? Not that my breasts had been small before, but now…none of my brassieres fit properly and I'd had to send to Singapore for more underthings. Luckily, Anne and Jackson had sailed with the *Islander* at the beginning of last week, and we expected their return any day now.

Sarah's impatience won and she seized the comb from my fingers, dragging it through my hair as if trying to carve my scalp with the teeth. Not like handing my comb to William, whose every stroke was a caress. Still, five minutes later, she'd pinned my hair up for me and we headed for the dining room where William waited.

I tucked into my lunch as if I were eating for two and I guess I was – two people as well as two meals, to make up for the breakfast I'd missed – letting William and Sarah talk. He spoke of the *Islander* docking while I slept, and the huge fish the coolies had caught fishing last night, now the monster shark had mysteriously disappeared. He moved restlessly in his seat, his eyes darting from his food to me and back to his plate, even when Sarah spoke. I wondered what news he'd received from the *Islander* that he couldn't share with Sarah and I. I didn't think it was bad news, as he seemed on the brink of blurting something out for most of the meal, yet when Amah took the empty plates from the table, his eagerness only increased, so he hadn't spilled his news yet.

Perhaps it was someone who'd arrived on the *Islander*, I guessed. Another of his relatives, or a dear friend. Anne and her husband were undoubtedly aboard, but their return home was hardly news.

I caught the faint chugging of an engine approaching – it sounded like William's motorcycle, but as he was here, the sound evidently heralded the arrival of Jackson, the acting island manager, on his ageing Triumph.

William threw his napkin on the table and rose, grinning widely. Was it Jackson's return he'd so eagerly awaited? Surely not.

"Sounds like the Jacksons are home. Care to come greet them, lass?" William held out his hand and curiously, I took it, letting him pull me outside. He left me in the shade of the veranda, trotting down the steps to meet Jackson as he pulled up in our garden.

Behind me, Sarah sidled out of the door, no less curious than I was. After all, she knew her brother and his excitement must have been just as obvious to her. "What is it?" she asked softly.

I shrugged. "Mr Jackson's returned, and it looks like he has a new motorcycle. This one's not rusted at all." More than not rusted – this one was black and shiny and completely unlike William's or Jackson's. Yet as I peered at the blue logo on the fuel tank, barely a shade lighter than my tail, I realised that this was also a Triumph…but a much newer model.

William stood beside the Triumph as Jackson dismounted, spreading his arms wide. "What do you think, lass?"

I want one, was my first thought. The second was that I needed to know more about riding one. A mermaid on a motorcycle was joke enough without me wobbling around with no idea of what I was doing.

"This model has twin-shoe brakes instead of the dummy-belt rim ones my Triumph has. And this has the new low-pressure, wire-edged tyres which won't jolt so much. The ride will be much smoother. The oil – "

Pregnancy must have dulled my wits, for Sarah understood better than I did. She stormed down the steps. "Will, you're a bloody fool! Buying your pregnant wife a motorcycle? What kind of crazed idea is that? You think she wants to ride that throbbing thing while she's carrying your child in her belly? You're a – "

Wonderful, wonderful man. I couldn't seem to speak the words. I just stared at him and the motorcycle, but mostly at him. William understood, though. Since the day we met on the *Trevessa*, he'd been reading my eyes and the thoughts behind them.

I stumbled down the steps, clutching at the handrail to slow my descent, my eyes never leaving William's. Once I stood on flat ground,

I threw myself into his arms, planting fervent kisses on his mouth, his cheeks and any part of his face I could reach.

Jackson's voice cut through my euphoria. "You mean this magnificent machine is for your wife? McGregor, you're crazy, man! My wife wouldn't touch one of these things, let alone know how to ride one. Or appreciate the engineering that went into creating it…" He stroked the curved fuel tank so fervently I wondered if he'd ever touched Anne that way. I doubted it. In fact, it was almost obscene.

"Mr Jackson, I'll thank you to stop fondling my motorcycle."

He flushed and backed away from it.

William chuckled. "So you like it, lass?"

I wanted to cover him in kisses all over again. Tonight, certainly. "Yes. Thank you so much, William. I can't wait for you to show me how to ride it." I dropped my voice so low only he could hear it. "And afterwards…" I let my eyes speak for me.

William wrapped his arms tightly around

me. "Good thing I have the rest of the afternoon off, then, with all the coolies unloading in the port instead of up the mine today. I think we should take your new baby for her first trip to the Grotto."

I laid a hand on my belly as my eyes strayed to my new, shiny toy, reflecting the noon sun. My loins already ached in anticipation. "Absolutely."

Two

I fastened the buttons on my leather jacket, surprised that the riding leathers I'd bought in Singapore still fit. Even the pants made it around my midsection, though they were a little snug. The soft feel of leather against my skin was sensual, driving my pregnancy-heightened senses to distraction. William would relieve my sexual tension when we reached the Grotto, I promised myself as I pulled on my leather gloves. These were ladies' gloves, unlike William's riding gloves, covering my hands to just past my wrists and flaring properly to still allow me freedom of movement. I even managed to pull on my boots without removing my gloves. And these were the sort of boots I'd only seen men wear, for I'd never owned boots so big. These didn't just cover my feet to the ankle – they encased my calves to just below my knees.

When I was done, I glanced in the mirror. For the first time in my life, I truly looked like a daughter of the Gold line, clad head to foot in golden brown from my felt hat to the toes of my boots. The absence of my tail flukes gave me away, though. Today, a mermaid would ride her first motorcycle, symbolic of my surrender to living my life solely on land with William.

I strode out to meet him.

Sarah rose from her seat on the veranda. "Maria, you really should reconsider. Think of your child and the danger —"

I shook my head. "She'll be fine. We both will be."

William grinned on the grass below, having heard our exchange, but when I stepped out of the shadow of the veranda, letting the sun light up my leathers, his expression glowed with admiration. He swallowed as if his mouth was dry, even as his eyes drank me in. "Lass, you look…magnificent."

Whatever I looked like, all I felt was nervous as I mounted my motorcycle. I ran my fingers over the curve of the fuel tank before I tentatively grasped the handlebars. "I can't remember what to do first," I admitted.

"Clutch," William said, nodding at my left hand.

I stared at the two levers. I knew one controlled the spark, so the other had to be the clutch. "What's it do?"

"It disconnects the gearbox so you can change gears."

"Oh! I always thought it was called the

crunch, because that's the noise Tony's truck made whenever he changed gears." I smiled ruefully.

William's smile had vanished. "A man who couldn't ride a motorcycle and couldn't drive a truck properly either. And he tried to steal you from me. Next time I'm in Fremantle, he won't get off so lightly with a few mud spatters."

"William. Forget about my old boss and everyone else. It's just you, me and this complicated machine." I stared at the levers in front of me and dropped my voice to a whisper. "Maybe Sarah's right and I should wait until after the baby's born. There's so much to learn and I can barely remember how to stir my tea any more."

"Where's my fearless lass? I thought you wanted to come with me to the Grotto for a romantic swim together. It isn't hard and I know you rode well the first time. You even enjoyed it." William's smile mirrored my own. "Can you remember which lever controls the spark?"

I tapped it without hesitation, adjusting it to the middle.

"Throttle, then air."

I opened the throttle lever up the tiniest bit, then fiddled with the air until William seemed satisfied.

"Fuel."

Cautiously, I released a little fuel until the stench of it assailed my nostrils.

"Now give it a kick."

I hadn't used the kickstart before – William had done it for me the first time. I touched my toes to it.

"You have to stamp on it like a giant spider you're afraid will bite you, lass."

I wasn't afraid of spiders. They responded to my voice as readily as crabs. And my Triumph was much bigger and heavier than even the robber crabs on the island. I shifted my foot so my heel rested on the kickstart lever and stomped down hard, as if I was trying to break a man's foot.

The engine coughed into life and I cheered.

"Now adjust the spark and the throttle until it sounds right." A hint of doubt had crept into William's voice. "Do you remember what it should sound like?"

He was asking a siren if she remembered her favourite song – the sound of her beloved returning home. And not just any siren, but possibly the most powerful singer in the Indian Ocean. Biting back my smile, I nodded.

Under my careful hands, my motorcycle assumed a perfect rhythm.

"Do you want me to lift the stand, or do you think you can do it? Just roll it forward a bit and…good. Lift it a bit with your foot and…ah, don't worry about it, lass. I'll hook it up out of your way." I heard the clink of metal on metal. "Do you know how to change gears?"

No. I searched the Triumph for some button or lever I'd missed. William's hand closed over my right hand and guided it to a knob beside the fuel tank. I clutched the clutch in my other hand and pulled on the knobbed gear-change lever.

"You're ready to go, lass. I'll ride beside you and remind you when to change gears. You're in the bottom gear at the moment, because we'll be headed up to the plateau before we take the track down to Waterfall. Now, do you remember how to speed up and how to stop?"

I tapped the throttle. "That one's to go faster. To stop…I make it slow down with this, then use the brakes." I touched the brake lever with the smallest finger on my right hand. "And the main brake's here, for my foot." My left boot grazed the pedal.

William's mouth claimed mine in a kiss that ignited my insides more effectively than the spark burning fuel beneath me. "You're a natural at this, lass, and you haven't forgotten a thing. Are you ready?"

I nodded once.

He jumped on his Triumph and kicked it to life, adjusting everything without even glancing at it. "Off you go, lass. I'll be right behind or beside you. Nice and slow to start…"

I released the clutch and opened up the throttle, lifting my boots up to the footboards. William's didn't have these – he made do with pegs.

"Watch the road, lass!"

In panic, I lifted my eyes from his powerful, leather-clad legs to the muddy track curving away in front of me. I had to touch my foot on the ground more than once to keep the bike upright as I wobbled around the curve, but I made it.

"Don't take your eyes off the road. Hitting a crab could cause you to lose control of your motorcycle and I wouldn't want you to get hurt."

I nodded and hunched my shoulders into the wind. Crabs might respond to a song, but machines wouldn't and I could hardly sing the whole way, warning creatures out of my path.

"We're about to level out now. Time to change gears up!"

I did as I was told and found myself flying again, just as I had the first time. William was right. I was his fearless lass and I loved this almost as much as I did him.

Three

I slowly released the clutch as my Triumph stuttered into silence. Unclenching my hands from the handlebars, I climbed stiffly off the motorcycle. I hadn't realised quite how tensely I'd been riding until now, when relaxing nearly sent me sliding bonelessly to the mud. William caught me around the waist before I could, though.

His warm kiss shot through me, bolstering me like a steel rod up my backbone.

"You rode beautifully, lass. I've never seen anyone maintain their balance so well on their first solo ride. You take my breath away, you're so perfect." Another kiss melted my insides as he pulled me against him. Warm leather against leather was almost as sensuous as skin on skin.

A quick glance told me we were alone at the Grotto. I could escape my leathers and lose myself in loving William for the afternoon. Still kissing him fiercely, I fumbled with the buttons on my jacket. Finally, the last one popped free and I tried to shrug the hot garment off, but it stuck to my skin. I growled in frustration.

William broke our kiss, laughing. "What are you trying to do, lass?" His eyes followed mine to the open front of my jacket. "My God, you're not wearing anything under that!" His hands slid inside my jacket, freeing my breasts. His fingers slid up over my shoulders, crushing my bare chest against him, and I managed to shed my jacket.

William's jacket was next, then his uncomfortably tight pants. He still stood in his shirt and drawers, watching me, as I peeled off my own leather pants.

He swore as he saw that I hadn't bothered donning any underwear beneath my pants, so I stood naked before him.

"You're overdressed, William."

He laughed and the remains of his clothes soon dangled from his handlebars.

I threw myself at him once again, twining my legs around his body to get closer still. We overbalanced and ended up in the grass, rolling and laughing as we kissed, then kissed again. Slowly, we joined, his body completing mine in a union so natural I never wanted to be apart from him again. Our lovemaking was leisurely, building to a bone-deep climax that made me scream, frightening the frigatebirds into flight from a nearby tree.

Afterwards, we held tight to each other, irritating the child in my belly between us until she aimed a feeble kick in William's direction.

"You're covered in mud and dirt, lass. We should go for a swim," William murmured, making no move to release me.

Reluctantly, I sat up and surveyed my body. He was right. I rose and sauntered to the entrance to the cave, feeling his eyes on me every step of the way.

I climbed down the cliff into the Grotto proper, letting the sun-warmed water caress my legs as I lowered myself in. It barely came to my waist, but it was deep enough to lie on the surface and float. I stretched out and kicked my legs up, seeing my belly rise in a distinct curve just above the surface. She was certainly growing in there, this daughter of ours.

"A strange way to thank the human for planting a child in your belly, but I suppose you felt it fitting. One more joining before you leave him. Men are so easily pleased."

I jumped to my feet at the sound of Mother's voice, just in time to glimpse movement in the tunnel that led to the lower cave. Her father's cave, where her cradle still hung.

"Did you spot the dragon, lass?" William appeared on the rock ledge above, grinning. He pointed at the tunnel entrance. "That's where I saw it, too."

"No, of course not," I replied instantly. "The only dragon in this pool is me. I've told you that before."

I heard Mother's soft laughter and the sound of skin on stone as she swam deeper into the tunnel and out of sight.

He slid down the cliff and splashed into the water beside me. "Your leathers certainly look like dragon skin, and you wore nothing underneath, for a dragon wouldn't. And if you're a dragon, then so's this little one." He patted my belly, then gave a little snort of laughter. "If we have a girl, we should call her Belinda. It was my grandmother's name and it means beautiful serpent or dragon in German, she said. Any girl of yours will be beautiful, dragon or not."

"What about Apalala?" I asked lightly. "That's what you called the dragon you thought you saw here. I'm pretty sure we conceived this child here at the Grotto, too, if not in the water."

William wrapped his arms around me, pulling my wet body against his. "We could make love in the water again, just like the first time."

Desire flamed, but I knew Mother was watching. The moment I let my guard down, she might hurt William. I wouldn't let her.

"I want to," I admitted, "but last time you wore me out so much that I nearly fell asleep on the ride home. I can't afford to fall asleep while I'm riding your lovely gift." I softened my refusal by adding, "And we still have tonight in our bed."

"There are some positions in that book of yours that we haven't tried yet," William mused, winking at me. He splashed water on himself, washing away the mud from our roll in the dirt above.

"True. Don't think I've finished thanking you for your gift, either," I insisted. Satisfied that I was clean enough to don my leathers once more, I pointed upward. "You go first. I might need your help climbing over that last bit at the top. I'm getting clumsier as this child grows."

William leaned over to kiss my belly before he started his climb.

I kept my eyes on him, but nothing stoppered my ears.

"Yes, send him away. It is time for your exile to end, child. Tonight you return home with me, along with the child you carry. Obedience has its rewards and yours will be rich indeed."

I didn't bother answering her. I owed her no obedience. Not any more. Nothing she could offer me could match my happiness with William and the approaching birth of our daughter. Mother could stay here and rot, for all I cared. I wouldn't be travelling anywhere with her. Not tonight, not ever.

Four

The judder of the Triumph's engine between my thighs only rattled me more on our ride home. Mother's presence had turned what should have been a pleasurable ride with my husband into something both sinister and sour. I threw my hat on the hall table as we entered the house, scattering pins but not caring. My leathers felt too constricting and Apalala moved uneasily inside me, like a school of startled fish.

When I reached our bedroom, I unbuttoned my pants quickly, peeling them back from my belly. I stared critically at my increasingly curvy silhouette in the mirror, knowing I wouldn't be able to wear these pants again until after she was born. I cupped the distinctive bump between my hands, wondering whether her blue eyes would be as deep as William's or as stormy as mine. In five months I'd know, but until the time came, I'd have to protect both her and William from Mother. She was the most respected Elder among my people, which meant the most powerful person in the Indian Ocean. I knew I had the courage to oppose her, but would I have the strength to fight an entire ocean when she turned them against me?

I crossed my arms over my chest, feeling terribly insignificant. Warm arms encircled me as William stepped in close behind me. I looked up at our reflections, meeting his eyes.

"Is there anything you can't do, my courageous lass?" he asked, kissing my neck.

What if I can't protect you? my heart cried out silently, but the admiration in his eyes said otherwise. His belief and trust gave me more courage than I knew I had, simply because he believed in me.

"How will you astonish me next?" he continued. His gaze raked my reflection. "If I help you out of your dragon-skin, can I finish what we started at the Grotto?" Slowly, he unbuttoned my jacket and helped me out of it. I leaned back against him and for the first time realised that he was naked. His chest and belly were hard against my back as his arms pulled me close. His powerful thighs framed mine in the mirror, the hair on them glowing golden in the late afternoon sun. "God, you're beautiful. I need to see all of you."

"Same," I whispered, stroking a hand down his side.

William laughed. "Men aren't beautiful, lass. We're handsome or strong, powerful or gentle, but never beautiful."

I stroked him again, harder. "You're all of those things, William. And more. I'm…lucky to have you. Fortune smiled on me the day you spotted me from the deck of the *Trevessa*, and every day since."

"You look more beautiful now than the day I met you." His hands dropped to my belly, caressing the curve that hid Apalala from us. "But I'll have to get these pants off to show you properly." William slid his hands into my pants, hooking his thumbs into the waistband so that as he ran his fingers down my bum and my legs, he dragged my pants down with them until he met my boots. With his help, all three were soon in a jumble on the floor and he rose to his feet to stand behind me again. "Shift your feet a little further apart, lass," he whispered.

I did as he asked, letting my curious eyes question his reflection, but he only smiled.

William lifted my arms, stretching them toward the wall until he planted my hands on either side of the mirror. "Brace yourself, lass."

I felt his need pressing against me and understood. "Oh, I'm ready. I have been since the Grotto, lad."

He chuckled. "I feel like a callow lad with you, unsure of myself half the time, but I promise you, I'm a man." He grasped my hips and eased inside me, slowly enough to make me count every inch. "All man."

"Mmm, yes." I couldn't look away from the unfathomable depths of his eyes. At the peak of each thrust, his smiled seemed to grow wider and the pace quickened just a little until I found myself pushing back against him with all my strength to hold him inside me just a little longer on each stroke. But even with his slow, steady rhythm, I could feel my release building. My breathing became panting and I closed my eyes to better focus on the myriad sensations coruscating through my body.

"Open them, lass, and look at us." I met his eyes in the mirror again and they were laughing. "Not me, us. Look at the incredible woman your husband is making love to." He drove me closer to the cliff edge, yet held me there, not letting me fall until I shared his vision.

Haloed in red-gold down, his arm slung across my pelvis, keeping my hips from thrusting forward at his pleasurable onslaught. A shallow soup-bowl of a belly rose above it, curving to the base of my bouncing breasts, both globes bobbing happily with each powerful thrust of his hips. My lips parted, as if to draw in breath and moan at the same time. My half-closed eyes took in my reflection while wanting to lose myself in William's loving embrace. And above my shoulder was William's beloved face, devouring every inch of me with his eyes as his body gave me so much more in return. A siren and a human man, united in mutual desire. Never to be parted. Never.

"Ready, lass? Don't look away." Mutely, I nodded as it felt like my body fractured around him, held together only by his arms and the power of his love. I rose up onto my toes, my mouth opening wide to hail the heavens with his name. And I did. By water, I did.

When he withdrew, covering my neck and back in kisses, I found I was shaking with the power of my incredible release. How did he make my body sing so sweetly? William had a sort of siren-song all his own, it seemed.

"I want to know how you do that," I whispered.

"Later I'll show you again. Right now, we need to wash up and dress for dinner, lass," he said, reaching for the water jug on the washstand.

"But I still need to thank you for the motorcycle," I insisted. "Once is hardly enough."

William appeared behind me, now clad in his drawers and a shirt. "Anything for you, lass. How about tonight we go through that book you like so much and see if we have time to try all our favourite positions before dawn? I do have a request, though." He blushed. "All that talk of water dragons and motorcycles at the Grotto has me thinking of how we made love on the back of my Triumph that time. You know, when you lay back, lifted your legs up…"

"Like a mermaid?" I said without thinking.

"Is that what you call it? Then yes. Tonight I'd like you to be my mermaid, if only for a little while. Will you be my mermaid, lass?"

I met his eyes. "I will for as long as you'd like me to be, William." I meant it, too. If only he knew.

Five

I managed to make it to the breakfast table just before William entered the house.

"You look as if you didn't get enough sleep last night, lass," he whispered, leaning down to kiss me, to Sarah's snort of disapproval. "I enjoyed every minute of our time together, but you shouldn't have exerted yourself so much if you needed your sleep."

I'd loved every moment of our lovemaking last night, too. Remembering the taste and the feel of him was one of the reasons I'd lain so long in bed after he'd left for work. "I can sleep this afternoon. Sarah will probably insist on it, anyway."

Sarah muttered her agreement as she gulped her coffee. She wasn't the most cheerful person in the mornings.

Amah brought in William's letters while Cook served breakfast.

With Sarah intent on her coffee and William's attention captured by the post, I was the only one who thanked Amah and Cook as they set my tea and eggs before me.

"A letter for you from Australia, lass." William passed the envelope to me.

I swallowed my mouthful of tea. "It must be Merry's reply to the letter I sent her in Singapore!" Without even glancing at the address, I tore it open.

And stopped as I read the typed letter. Merry didn't own a typewriter, nor would she bother being so formal as to call me Mrs McGregor. The letter wasn't from her at all, I realised as I leafed through the pages, but some solicitor called Raphael D'Angelo. A relative of hers, I presumed. I turned back to the first page, resolving to read the missive from the beginning.

Four lines down, I burst into tears.

"What is it, lass? Does your aunt have bad news?"

I choked back a sob. "My aunt…Merry doesn't have any news at all. She died last winter, just after I left on the *Islander*. She had pneumonia. The bad cough she had was pneumonia and she died in her bed."

Tears flooded down my cheeks, blurring the breakfast table from my sight as William's warm arms enfolded me. "I'm so sorry, lass. Sorry I never met her." I heard the rustle of paper. "Why such a long letter, though?"

"I don't know," I mumbled through my tears. "You read it if you want to. I don't want sympathy from some stranger. I'd prefer to mourn her memory without reading any more. She died alone and I should have been there. Could have saved her, maybe…"

"It was her time, lass. No one can live past their time," Sarah said sadly. A light hand patted mine and I knew it was hers. "What more can we ask than to go gently and quickly in our sleep?"

"She named you her heir," William said.

Of course Mother had named me her heir. She wanted me to go back to Cocos and lead an ocean full of bloody-minded mermaids against humans, most likely. Well, she could die waiting. I didn't want to inherit the damn Indian Ocean and I wouldn't accept it. Not even if she begged. My heart froze in my chest. What if she'd killed Merry? Smothered her as she slept…

"Your aunt, Meryl D'Angelo, left everything she owned to you. To Maria Speranza McGregor. It says so in her will. Her house in Fremantle and everything in it. They're all yours now." William pressed the papers into my hands. "Read it, lass. Her will is dated the day the *Islander* sailed. Your aunt knew you'd find me and that we'd…so she named you her sole heir. You or your children."

I dabbed at my streaming eyes with my napkin and focussed on the papers before me. Mr D'Angelo's neatly typed letter spelled out just what William had said. Page after page detailed Merry's possessions – she'd owned our house and the school next door, too, with its extensive grounds. Money in the bank, as well. Merry hadn't been poor. She could have lived comfortably off the rent from the school alone, without working there as a teacher. And she'd left it all to me – someone not even of her blood, though I knew she had family. Her solicitor, for a start.

"You should go to Fremantle to meet with this solicitor and claim your inheritance," Sarah said. "Before you grow too close to your time to travel. The *Islander* is still in the port. We can take ship before it leaves and – "

"I'm not leaving William!" I interrupted,

aghast. Not with Mother here. Water only knew what she'd do to him if I disappeared.

"Sarah's right, though, lass. You should go to Fremantle for the birth. Christmas Island is no place for a baby. You have a house there, Sarah can stay with you, you know the place well and are comfortable there."

"And the heat here," Sarah piped up. "It's oppressive enough now, but when you're seven or eight months along, you'll find it quite unbearable, I'm sure. The climate is cooler in Fremantle. I'm sure you said it was."

"I'm only four months along yet," I protested. "At seven or eight months, maybe I'll agree to go, if I'm as uncomfortable as you say. But not without William."

Sarah opened her mouth to protest, but William waved her into silence. "Of course, lass. You have time to make up your mind. And if you want me to travel with you, of course I will."

I breathed a sigh of relief. I'd already lost Merry – William was all I had left in this world.

I wouldn't lose him. Not now, not ever.

Six

By afternoon, I'd managed to stem the tide of my mourning tears for Merry and I meekly agreed to go to bed at Sarah's insistence. Once the bedroom door was shut, I didn't head for the bed. I took my writing materials from my trunk and set them out on the desk by the window. If Merry had chosen to give me all her possessions, then I would honour her gift by ensuring it was well cared for. I'd never understood her motivation for helping me and now I never would. Why adopt a shipwrecked young woman, teach her to speak, read and write, give her a home, find her a job and offer her affection and good advice at every turn…if I believed in such things, I'd wonder if Merry was one of the angels they spoke of in her church. Or the book of fairy tales she'd given me, where mermaids aspired to be heavenly creatures.

I sat down and wrote a letter to Mr Raphael D'Angelo, solicitor, thanking him for contacting me and telling him to lease the house as he had the school for all these years. I couldn't live there again until my memories of Merry faded and that would be a long time coming. In the meantime, someone would have to maintain the property and whatever rents it brought in should be sufficient for that. I asked him to ensure that all of Merry's things were packed in tea chests – we had plenty of those on the back veranda, courtesy of Merry's and my taste for tea — and carefully stored for my eventual return.

I copied Mr D'Angelo's address carefully onto an envelope and sealed my letter inside. Tucking a hat over my hair without glancing at the mirror, so I wouldn't see my reddened, swollen eyes, I strode out of the bedroom with the letter clutched in my gloved hand. "I'm just going out for a walk!" I called.

"Yes, Mem," Cook replied. Sarah didn't say a thing — perhaps she'd already gone to visit Anne.

I set out along the track to the post office past the port, carefully nodding and smiling in response to the greetings I received from those I met along the way. No one dared to mention my tearstained appearance and I was grateful for it. At least the silly hierarchy here had some benefits.

I stopped in the shade of a tree by the port, turning my face to the salt breeze carrying coolness from the ocean. Were there dolphins in the cove today, spying for my mother? Did I care any more? She knew I was here and she knew about my pregnancy. If she hurt William or my child, I'd make her regret ever birthing me.

"Good day, Mrs McGregor," an English voice called from behind me and I scanned the coffee gardens, looking for the source of it. Captain Hughes stepped out of the shade and inclined his head. "I hope I find you well." He seemed to register my less than happy appearance and averted his eyes from my face.

My temper flared. "Good afternoon, Captain Hughes. I'm perfectly well. Glowing, or so my husband says, for we're expecting a child. And you?"

He congratulated me and made a non-committal response about the state of his own health. He looked as pensive as I felt, though.

"When does the *Islander* return to Singapore?" I asked politely.

His forehead creased deeper. "First, we're headed to Fremantle. My wife has had enough of the tropics and she insists on settling somewhere cooler, trading Singapore for Fremantle. This is our first voyage south this year, and she brought the children with her. I'll have four days in Fremantle to find them a new home before I'm due to return here. And that's if there aren't any delays, which there surely will be." He glanced into the shade he'd appeared from and I realised that Mrs Hughes and her children were within earshot on a picnic blanket on the grass. She looked just as worried as her husband, but the set of her mouth told me she wouldn't back down. Sarah would see me out of the tropics and back in Fremantle, too, with the child inside me. But Fremantle would be empty without Merry…

"I have an empty house in Fremantle," I blurted out. "One that needs a tenant. My aunt died and left it to me, but I can't travel at the moment to see the house packed up and let. I need someone I can trust to place my aunt's things in storage so that I can rent the place out." My eyes met those of Mrs Hughes. She didn't look a day older than me, but her years showed on her face while mine remained as youthful as the day I boarded the *Trevessa*.

She rose stiffly and walked to her husband's side. "My condolences for your loss. I'd be honoured to help you, Mrs McGregor. It's small thanks for already knowing we'll have a place to stay." She dropped an awkward curtsey.

"If you have writing paper and a pen, I'll add a postscript to my aunt's solicitor now, telling him you're my preferred tenants. If you'll deliver my letter personally, of course. I don't know how long it will take by post." I managed a weak grin.

Twenty minutes later, it was done. Mrs Hughes tucked my letter into her writing case as her husband swallowed, looked nervous and promised that everything would be taken care of…and could I please assure my husband of that?

I remembered his well-placed fear of William and agreed to mention it. Perhaps if William and Sarah knew Merry's house was already in good hands, they wouldn't be so insistent that I had to go there.

48

Seven

I woke in William's arms the next morning, my head aching from so many tears yesterday.

"Will you be all right today, lass? Sarah will stay with you, but if you need me, so will I. They can continue construction of the new pier without me for a day." He resumed rhythmically stroking my hair.

"I think I cried myself out yesterday,

William. I just…feel so guilty. Haring off after you when I should have stayed home to take care of her. She would've wanted to know that I was happy with you, too, that I found you and…now she'll never know."

"It's not your fault. Sarah's right about that. You're no doctor, lass. And I'm sure if she's the good person you say she was, she does know you're happy. She'll be looking down from her afterlife, secure in the knowledge that with her help, you found happiness, too. And she'll know all about little Belinda…"

I sat up, squinting at his face in the dim, pre-dawn light. "You truly think that? It's not just a fairy story? That death is not an end but some part of us lives on?"

William chuckled. "Of course I do, lass. I believe in ghosts, don't I, because I thought yours haunted me for years. Your body dies and your soul goes on. Maybe to a better place, or to haunt those responsible."

My heart lightened a little. "Merry isn't haunting me. I had no idea she was dead until I received the letter. That means…that means she doesn't blame me for her death."

His arms tightened around me. "She can't blame you. You were on the *Islander* the day she died, haunting me, or so I thought. It's not your fault. Simply…her time." He took a deep breath, his chest rising beneath my cheek. "If…if my time comes before yours, lass, I have a favour to ask."

His…time? William wasn't pregnant. Realisation dawned. "No. Don't even say it. You won't die before me. I won't let you!" I'd fight Mother myself to protect him. Fight every fish in the ocean with my voice and my body and every scrap of strength I owned.

"Easy, lass. No one can fight their time when it comes. Not even you, though I suspect death would have its hands full trying to take you. I just…seeing how heartbroken you were yesterday and all those tears that I'd have given anything to stop. I felt so helpless. I can repair a pier, a railway line, a ship…but your broken heart was beyond me. And if my time came…God forbid, but if it did…I don't know how I could bear to see your pain and not be able to comfort you any more. If fate forces me to leave you, rail at me. Vent your fury on me for leaving you alone. But don't cry for me. I can't bear the thought of…of…" He swore as he realised his words had already brought tears to my eyes.

If I failed to protect him and Mother killed him, his death would be my fault. I swore by everything I held dear, by my own life, that I wouldn't let that happen. "William, I've already lost one husband. And I remember that it didn't matter whether my eyes were dry as a desert or if I cried a new ocean, still the pain in my heart remained. And Giuseppe…my love for him is but a faint whisper of what I feel for you. If I lose you, my heart would shatter into a million razor-sharp shards that will swim in my bloodstream, piercing me over and over with the pain of my smashed heart. Don't…don't talk about it, please. And you take care at work today. Today and every day, so that I never have to endure the agony of losing you."

Cook came to the door then and told him that his tea was ready, stealing William from me so he could start work for the day.

Eight

William didn't return for breakfast, which happened often now he was working on the pier. The original one had been swept away in a summer cyclone and he swore his design would withstand even the fiercest swells in Flying Fish Cove. I didn't doubt it. He was so proud of the project, he got carried away working on it and forgot to eat. If the coolies didn't insist on finishing work at the end of the day, he'd have worked long into the night, too.

I wrapped some toast and muffins in a napkin to take to William and joined Anne and Sarah for what had become our regular morning walk down to the port to see the progress on William's pier.

Today when we arrived, the men were all lined up along the beach beside the lighters they used to carry the materials to the bottom of the pier, with only a few on the structure itself, peering over the edge at the water below. My heart lurched and I pushed my way through the throng to stand on the wet sand. A commotion beneath the pier drew my attention and I blinked, doubting my own eyes. The water was alive with a veritable frenzy of sharks, fighting one another, leaping into the air and thunking against the struts. More than one of the metal beams bore kinks and dents from the fierce fighting, for several of the sharks were ten or fifteen feet long. I scanned the surface for the body causing their frenzy, for surely something had to have incited their aggression, but all I saw was blood in the water and a few shreds of what might be floating flesh. Then my gaze travelled up the pier and I gasped.

Hanging halfway up the structure, just above the waves, was a tiger shark bigger than all the rest. He – it was a male – looked close to twenty feet long and his innards spilled out of a gouge in his belly that ran from his tail up to his jaw. The big hook from the winch above was buried deep inside the eviscerated carcass, suspending the whole gory mess over his voracious, snapping brethren.

The men behind me whispered, wondering who had fished up the monstrous shark. A human could have done it, with the right bait, quick reflexes and a whole lot of luck, but I knew no human would be crazy enough to venture into the water to fasten the winch hook into the body before hoisting it up. For a human, it would be tantamount to suicide.

A pod of dolphins could have killed a shark

this big, but none of them could have operated the winch. Only one of my kind could call such a powerful shark, slaughter it and walk on land to winch it up as a grisly decoration on the new port infrastructure.

And who among my kind would play such a pointless prank?

Mother. But she hadn't meant it to be pointless at all. Her purpose was to convey a warning to me…about William.

I'd have to return to the Grotto and speak to her, telling her that I wasn't interested in returning to Cocos with her. And if she harmed William…

I glimpsed a sapphire-blue ripple that was no wave and no shark, either. Mother's head rose to the surface and her eyes met mine. I nodded slightly, jerking my head to the east where the Grotto was.

She nodded and sank out of sight.

This afternoon, I'd pay the Grotto a visit. Without William.

Nine

I waited until William had returned to work before I announced my intentions to Sarah: "I'm going for a swim."

"Swimming? Cold water isn't good for the baby and remember what happened last time you and Will went out in the cove." Sarah's frown deepened. "It's probably still full of sharks. And you've just finished lunch! You should wait until Will returns and see what he says."

William would flatly refuse to let me anywhere near the cove, I knew, though the sharks posed no danger to me.

"I'm not going to the cove. I'll go to the Grotto, the cave near Waterfall where William and I swim together sometimes. There aren't any sharks there. In fact, there's not even any salt in the cave pool."

She still looked doubtful. "How far is it?"

I shrugged "A few miles."

"You can't walk that far in nothing but your bathing suit!" she exclaimed in horror.

For a moment, I wished I could tell her that I'd prefer to swim the distance naked.

"I won't. I'll take my Triumph, like William and I usually do. I know the way. There's only one track and it goes straight there. I'd have to be a complete idiot to get lost." I felt like a complete idiot as I pulled on my boots, hat and gloves, leaving the rest of my leathers at home, but I couldn't fasten my leather pants around the ruffled bathing suit. Stretching it across my thickened waist had been challenge enough.

As always when Sarah lost an argument, she fired the same parting shot: "But think of the risk to your baby."

I clipped the stand to the rear mudguard and mounted my motorcycle. "She'll enjoy the swim. She usually kicks less when I'm in the water. And I feel better for floating because I can't feel her weight."

I could feel the weight of Sarah's disapproval as she frowned at my back, but I shoved the thought to the back of my mind. This was to protect William. And I'd need all my flighty mind's focus on the motorcycle because William wouldn't be here to help me if I forgot what to do.

Casting my memory back to our last ride to the Grotto, I listed the start sequence under my breath as I touched each lever. "Clutch, spark? Throttle, then air. Fuel." I wrinkled my nose as I smelled it, then lifted my boot to stomp the engine into life. "Kickstart. Adjust the spark and the throttle until it sings. Stand." I glanced at the stand, which was firmly fastened to the mudguard. "Gear. And off we go." I opened up the throttle as I released the clutch.

The Triumph thrummed between my legs, carrying me out of Sarah's sight around the bend. I breathed a sigh of relief as I relaxed and simply enjoyed the ride.

All too soon I arrived at the Grotto, cruising to a stop more smoothly than I had the first couple of times. William would be proud, I thought as I allowed myself a small smile of triumph. I draped my hat, gloves and boots over the seat and contemplated adding the bathing suit, too, so I could shift to my tail. No, I decided. I'd set Mother on edge with my human appearance instead. After all, I'd come to tell her that I'd chosen a life with legs on land.

I luxuriated in the sun-warmed water in the Grotto pool for a few minutes before I drew in a deep breath and plunged into the tunnel. One of my ruffles caught on the rough stone and ripped, but I continued swimming. I could blame it on the climb back up the cliff, if anyone at home asked.

She waited for me in the water below, but I ignored her as I made my way to the rock ledge that I'd used for a bed when this cave was my home. Cold and hard compared to my life with William. Why in water would I want to come back to this? Mother was crazy if she thought I would.

I perched on the edge of the ledge, kicking my feet through the water as if I didn't have a care in the world. "The shark was careless, Mother. What would the Elder Council say if they knew you flaunted our existence in front of hundreds of humans?" I realised I'd spoke in English and repeated the words in our own language of sound and gesture. The high-pitched squeaks I emitted echoed around the cave, a cacophony of distorted mermaid voices the like of which I hadn't heard in almost a decade. And I found I didn't miss it.

"None of them saw me. And it got your attention." Her gestures flowed with a familiarity that mine lacked.

Had I forgotten the language of my own people so readily in my time on land? I should have felt shame or sadness at the loss, but I found it gave me satisfaction. It was easier to live like a human when I thought like one.

Mother stretched out on the surface, so her flukes extended beneath my toes. Cream over sapphire blue, the colour of William's eyes. *"I could have used your human lover to decorate the cove instead, but I was unsure if you were finished with him yet. Besides, your assassination skills are not in question. Not after you slayed your first lover before you even knew you carried his child. Your kill count is impressive for one so young."*

As if I'd meant to kill those aboard the *Emden* or the *Sydney*. Or Giuseppe, whose life I'd tried to save, not take. *"If you so much as touch William, I will kill YOU."*

She laughed. *"You presume to command me,*

child? I rule the Elder Council of the Indian Ocean. No one dares to disobey me." Her eyes flashed dangerously and I fought down my fear. It wouldn't do to show weakness in front of her, for she'd spot it instantly.

I reclined against the wall, pretending it was a comfortable cushion instead of cold, unyielding rock. "Yet I have not obeyed you for a decade or more and I have no intention of doing so now. Do the Elder Council know your secret?" I stabbed a finger at her name carved into the wall. "So much for the Elder of the Gold line. You are as black as your heart, and so am I."

"It does not matter who my father was. None of the ocean's gift in this ocean can trace a clearer line of Gold ancestry than I can." Mother's expression was smug. "I made sure of that when Mother showed me this cave."

"I thought Zarrineh and her daughters died in the Krakatoa eruption north of here. At least, that is what Duyong told me. The lesson for that story is that subsea vents are to be avoided at all costs." I eyed Mother. "Are you saying you caused the explosion, or were you merely responsible for sending Zarrineh there to investigate it when you knew it was unsafe?"

"The Gold line are known for their pride, as the Black line are known for their ruthlessness in battle. I mentioned to Zarrineh that Mother and I had seen glowing stone beneath the ocean's surface. She denied its existence and I told her to ask Mother or go and see it for herself. Her twin daughters were training in geology, so they accompanied her." Mother's eyebrows rose. "I simply neglected to tell her that the dissolved fumes from the vent were as poisonous as a cone shell. She was the stone expert, after all. Surely an expert would know such things."

Not if she'd never seen molten volcanic rock before, I fumed. Much like Mother sending me ashore without knowing a word of English or even the basic customs of the people I intended to seduce. Stupid and short-sighted. How were our people to survive if they were guided by the likes of her? They were doomed and they wouldn't take me down with them.

"A good leader would not waste valuable people in the heedless pursuit of personal power," I blurted out.

Mother stared at me and I realised I'd never heard this from her in her interminable lectures on leadership. I'd learned from watching William in his dealings with Captain Hughes and his subordinates. Hughes wouldn't be alive today if William was the same sort of leader as Mother.

"They were a threat to me, to Duyong, to you – " she began.

"Shark shit, Mother. I was not even born yet." I heard her shocked gasp, but continued, "A good leader holds power through personal strength, communication and charisma. Building relationships, defusing situations before they explode and not through pissing people off!" I forced myself to smile. "Does the Council know what you are doing here?"

Mother lost her temper. "Bringing you home, you ungrateful, disobedient child!"

My heart froze in my chest, but I widened my smile to hide the chill. "I am not a child. Nor was I a child when you exiled me, a fact you seem to have forgotten. And what do I have to be grateful for? That you stole my daughter and turned me out of the only home I had ever known, without the knowledge I would need to survive in the human world? Make no mistake, Mother. Humans own this world and one day they will own the oceans, too. As for disobedient…what power do you hold over me any more? I cannot think of a single thing I should do for you. Except tell you that if you string sharks up in the cove again, I will tell the humans you were responsible for it. And they will hunt you."

Her mouth gaped in shock. "You cannot. To share the secret of our existence with humans…you would have to kill them all!"

I laughed. "Mother, you saw what I did to the Emden as a child. Do not underestimate my powers now I am grown. I can bend every human on this island to my will, and kill them if I must." My insides writhed in horror at the thought, but I firmed my expression to hide the turbulence beneath the surface.

Suspicion narrowed her eyes and I knew I'd failed. "You do not enjoy killing, however skilled you are. Come home with me now and I will leave the humans here alone."

"An empty offer, Mother. You must leave them alone anyway, or risk exposing yourself for what you are, while I move freely among them." I moistened my mouth, wishing for a cup of tea. Surely it was afternoon tea time at home – I could mount my motorcycle and be home in a matter of minutes. Suddenly the etiquette of a formal afternoon tea seemed a lot more logical than anything Mother had to say.

"What about your lover? He surely knows what you are and for that his life is forfeit," she taunted, her eyes sparkling as if she tasted victory.

"You underestimate me, Mother. He is as ignorant of our kind as the other humans on the island." Except that he'd once seen my tail and thought me a dragon, I thought, turning to go so she wouldn't catch my consternation. If William came to the Grotto and saw Mother, she'd have an excuse to kill him to preserve our secret. I had to keep him from the Grotto at all costs, then, I resolved, swimming for the tunnel to the surface.

"He will no longer be ignorant when he sees his child. Your daughter will be one of us, and you will not be able to hide it. Your time on land is limited by the baby you carry. It is a long swim to the Birthing Grounds, and your time is running out, child." Her hollow laugh echoed in the cave below. "You will come to me before it is your time. I know it."

The fingers of fear closed into a fist around my heart as I broke the surface in the Grotto pool. Sunlight couldn't warm me as shivers wracked my body, but I kicked my Triumph into life and set off before Mother emerged to taunt me further.

William couldn't be allowed to see her, and what would I do about our child? If she was born with a tail, as Mother said she would be, I couldn't hide it from him. Or Sarah, if she was my midwife for the birth.

The motorcycle whined and I quickly shifted gears to quiet it. I could contemplate solutions later, I decided. I had three months before I'd have to set out for the long swim to Cocos, if I had to go there. Three months to find a solution that would allow William and I to stay together with our baby girl. And I would – for his life depended on it.

Ten

I pushed the Triumph harder than I ever had before, opening the throttle up completely and letting the jungle on either side of me blur as I revelled in the speed. I needed to regain my calm before William came home from work because he'd know something was wrong the moment he looked at me. And how could I tell him the truth?

The tyres squealed to a stop in the front yard and I jumped off, setting the motorcycle on its stand. I peeled my hat from my head and glanced down at my mud-spattered body. So much for a relaxing swim. I needed a bath.

I stumbled for the veranda, but the sound of running footsteps behind me made me turn.

"What were you thinking?" William shouted, his eyes wild. "Riding on your own. And going so fast. What if you'd hit something?" He grabbed my shoulders.

I lifted my eyes to meet his. "I went to the Grotto for a swim. I thought the breeze would dry my bathing costume better on the way back if I rode faster."

His fingers dug into my shoulders as his grip tightened. "You can't go riding on your own. It's too dangerous. You hear me? I won't let you!"

I jerked out of his grasp. He didn't know a thing about danger. "I heard you, but I'm going to pretend I didn't. I can ride just fine on my own."

He waved at the mud turning my blue bathing suit brown. "Fine? Fine? Where'd all the mud come from if you didn't fall off? Did you even think about the damage you could do to our baby?"

After all of Mother's antagonism, added to my worry for William and Apalala's birth, I snapped. "I didn't fall off!" I roared. "The track was wet from last night's rain and I ran through a couple of big puddles. Without falling off. I won't be kept prisoner in your house, William. I'm not some delicate flower you need to press between the leaves of a book. And nor is this baby. You'll LET me do what I damn well please."

"And then what? You'll go riding dangerously all over the island without me, so when something happens I won't be there to save you? I won't lose you again, lass. And I won't let you hurt our baby. Tonight I'll take your Triumph apart and – "

"Save me? Since when do I need you – or ANY man – to save me? I lived in the jungle here just fine when – " I broke off quickly before I blurted out anything I shouldn't. Instead, I said, "And who saved who when we went fishing? You capsized the bloody boat and knocked yourself out. If I hadn't dragged you to shore, you're the one who would've drowned. I wanted a swim and I went to the Grotto so you wouldn't worry about me swimming in the cove with sharks. Next time, I'll just dive off the damn pier or take one of the kolaks out by myself or – "

Sarah shoved between us, her eyes wide with fright. "Lass, don't make it worse. Will, she's your wife. Your wife. She's in a delicate condition, carrying your child. She made a mistake. I'll keep her home and make sure she stays safe. Don't – "

William the wifebeater. She still believed it, even after living with us and not seeing him raise a hand to me. Sick of the whole McGregor family, I turned and trotted up the steps to the house.

"Where are you going? We're not done

talking!" William shouted. His pounding steps shook the veranda.

"Your not-so-delicate wife needs a bath. You can come and shout at me there if you want. I'll stick my head under the water when I've heard enough." I threw my hat, gloves and hairpins on the floor as I walked in a bathing suit and knee-high boots to the bathroom.

Amah ducked her head as I entered. "Your bath is running, Mem." She sidled through the doorway and escaped before William burst in and closed the door behind him with a click of finality.

I sat on the edge of the bath and tugged at my left boot, but it was stuck fast. The right was much the same. I swore and shed my bathing costume, then stepped into the bath, boots and all. I held one under the tap and then the other, filling them with water before sliding them off and throwing them onto the floor.

Then I turned the water off and let the bath drain as I stood facing William, waiting.

He licked his lips, desire plain in his expression. "I won't lose you. I'll do anything to keep you safe."

"I'd do the same for you, William." I wrenched at the tap and plugged the bath again.

He dropped to his knees. "Please, lass. I love you and I'll protect you and our child any way I can. I'm begging you not to do those things. I'll go mad with worry. If anything happened to you, I'm not sure I could live with myself. I've lost you once. I won't lose you again."

I closed my eyes. "I'll do it if you will. Promise me you won't go swimming with sharks, fishing by yourself or swimming at the Grotto alone."

"You have my word, lass. Anything else?" His relieved smile was the first real sunshine on this otherwise dark day.

"Yes. Take your clothes off and come here."

He'd already shrugged out of his shirt before he said, "It's the middle of the afternoon. Don't you think it's a bit early for…"

I eyed his pants. "No. And nor do you. We can break for dinner. Maybe even get dressed."

Eleven

I sucked in a breath, tensing as William pushed me over the brink into bliss before I screamed.

"Too much for you, lass?" he whispered, not breaking his slow rhythm for a moment.

"No," I tried to say, but my voice failed. I swallowed and tried again. "No!" It came out louder than I'd expected.

Someone started knocking on the bedroom

door.

William cursed.

"Don't...stop..." I panted, then turned to shout at the closed door: "Leave us alone!"

William grinned. Fastening his hands tightly around my hips, he rolled and pulled me on top of him, matching the movement with a particularly powerful thrust.

I moaned and threw my arms out to maintain my balance, knocking something off the nightstand. Books cascaded to the floor in a series of thumps. I didn't care. All that mattered was William.

He sat up, pressing his lips to my breast as his thrusts slowed. He was close – I recognised the signs – and he knew my body better than I did, so I'd reach my peak with him. Already my nerves crackled with anticipation.

Deep in, then an agonisingly slow withdrawal before he filled me once more. One more...just one...and a second scream ripped from my throat, harmonising with William's groan as he finished deep inside me.

I kept my eyes closed as I held onto the fading sensations still shaking my body, but the odd feeling of William winding a sheet around my torso made me open them quickly. Why in water would he want me covered up when we'd just made love?

"Are…are you all right?" Sarah squeaked.

I glanced over my shoulder. William's sister stood in the wide open doorway, clutching at her pale face. Now I understood why William had tried to cover me.

I couldn't seem to wrap my tongue around a response. The words fine and well weren't appropriate for the fierce fizzing in my blood when William still filled me.

William chuckled. "You didn't pick the best time to intrude, Sarah. She's still breathless." His mouth claimed mine and I responded to his kiss as if his breath was all the air I needed. Two…three, four kisses, before I found my voice.

"I'm fine." Such inadequate words for my feelings.

Her voice trembled. "You…you told him to stop. To leave you and the baby alone. I heard blows…"

I peered blearily at the floor, where the stack of books on the nightstand had landed. "I told him not to stop, and you to leave us alone."

"He beat you. I'm sure of it. You screamed!"

Inwardly, I cursed the human prudery that forbade me from telling her the plain truth. My reticence lasted for barely a moment before I threw caution to the current. "If what we do together is what you call a beating in Scotland, then I'll take it and ask for more." I pressed my cheek to William's chest, where I rejoiced at his racing heartbeat. "Your brother is the sort of lover most women dream about, but never know." I waved at my belly. No amount of sheet could hide the swell of it. "Why do you think I fell pregnant so quickly?"

William coughed. I was surprised to find his face flushed red from more than exertion. "Excuse me, ladies." I winced as he withdrew from me, wrapping another sheet around his body like one of the Malay men's sarongs. He padded out in the direction of the bathroom.

Sarah couldn't seem to take her eyes off me. I shifted into a more comfortable sitting position, now that William wasn't between my thighs, and settled the sheet to preserve my non-existent modesty for Sarah's benefit. "Sarah, if your brother tried to beat me, I'd match him bruise for bruise. And he wouldn't be capable of – " Making love to me like it was our last night together. " – what we just did. Have you ever seen your brother in a fight?"

She pressed her lips together, as if she was weighing her response. Finally, she lowered her eyes and nodded.

"Me, too. And only once did I see him lose."

She stared at me in horror. "He fought YOU?"

I shook my head slowly. "Of course not. He fought two men who had…said unkind things about me. Then a man challenged him for a wager. A very experienced Japanese fighter.

William went down."

"Will always won. He never lost a fight, even against the bigger boys. He was the best fighter, always."

"Kaito was better. William wouldn't…wouldn't let the fight end, though he was injured. So I stepped into the ring." I met her horrified eyes. "I won the bout against Kaito. His was a different style of fighting to what you have in Scotland, I think. More agility and calculation than force, which gave me the advantage. Even if William tried to strike me – and he hasn't, not once – he would struggle to land a blow."

"But the bruises. I saw the bruises in Singapore…"

It was my turn to lower my eyes. "The afternoon rain turned the marble floors as slick as ice and my illness made me clumsy. William managed but I simply couldn't. Ice on the ground is not something I'm used to." I thought of the only ice I'd known and laughed. "Well, except when the crabs tipped the bucket over in the fish market. Then we had ice everywhere and the silly creatures to catch again, too. But they were never my crabs, so I could stand back and watch, if I wanted." I winked. "Nothing's more entertaining than a group of rugged fishermen crawling around on their hands and knees trying to grab creatures that were just as aggressive and happy to nip tender bits in their claws."

She stared at me, evidently struggling to find an appropriate reply. Finally, she said, "Did you really rescue Will when your boat capsized?"

I nodded. "We weren't far from shore," I explained, then closed my mouth before I had to tell her how many miles constituted close to land for one of my kind.

"I don't think you're as young as you look," she said. Two bright spots appeared on her cheeks.

"I'm twenty-seven years old," I stated wearily. "I've been shipwrecked twice, widowed once, and lost all of my family.

Including my daughter." I caught sight of the tears trickling down Sarah's cheek and broke off.

"Does Will know?" she whispered urgently.

"Not about my daughter. Don't tell him, please," I implored.

Her expression turned thoughtful. "That depends. Did she die at birth or during some complication? If you can't bear children, you should tell him."

I shook my head. "No. She was born perfect. It wasn't until she was two years old that…that…" My murderous mermaid of a mother ripped her from my arms and banished me from her life. I wrapped my arms around my belly. I wouldn't be parted from this child the same way. Mother would feed the sharks before I let her touch William's little water dragon.

Twelve

"Drink, Mem?" A child whose head barely reached the arm of my cane chair lifted a cup into the air, tilting it at an alarming angle that almost spilled the contents down her back.

"Thank you." I rescued the cup from the Malay girl and sipped. Fresh, young coconut water filled my mouth, and I nodded my thanks to the girl's mother, who stood under the shade of a coconut-fibre-thatched atap roof on the other side of the football field.

Well, it was our tennis court in truth, but Anne's son Alan had insisted he needed to practice football before he went to school in Scotland after Sarah had said how good her own son was at the game. So the kampung boys (and some girls) had been conscripted and Sarah had explained the rules as young Alan translated.

A piercing whistle lanced across the field and the tired children trooped off into the shade for a mid-match drink. Sarah flopped into the chair beside me. "Refereeing these games makes me miss my own sons. All three of them are at school, but when they were home for the holidays, they'd play from dawn until dusk. I wish I had the energy." She nodded at my midsection. "You just wait until that one's out. You won't believe the energy they have when they start running."

I smiled and rested my cup lightly on top of my bulging belly. Apalala promptly kicked it and we both laughed. "Just over two months to go. It can't come fast enough. I feel like a whale already. A beached one. But I think if I managed to get into the water, I wouldn't be able to get out again, so I'll be a whale right here for a while longer yet."

"Will would pull you out," she said, rising. Sarah stuck her fingers in her mouth and whistled shrilly again. "Second half!"

Perhaps, but he'd need a winch. I'd grown so heavy even he couldn't lift me any more. I hadn't felt this huge with my first daughter, but then I'd been buoyed up by the ocean for the whole of my first pregnancy. Not dragging my feet on land.

I slipped into a light doze as the game resumed, jerking my eyes open when Sarah whistled at rule breakers, before sinking back into slumber. Apalala took so much of my energy, sapping my strength – or so it seemed. There was no way now that I could manage the long swim to Cocos. Mother wouldn't be able to tear me away from William no matter how hard she tried. It'd be like trying to control a deaf orca.

Quiet, male voices roused me. "How long has it been since you played football, McGregor?"

"Since that match where you blocked the penalty with a kick so high the other team cried foul," William replied, laughing. "They wouldn't have if they'd ever seen you fight."

"I still can't believe the dean made me resign from the team after that. None of their goalkeepers were up to scratch after I left."

"I bet I could best you now, though."

The unfamiliar Englishman chuckled. "You're on, McGregor."

I turned my head to regard the men. William's expression softened into an instant smile but my eyes widened when I caught sight of the other man. He didn't look like an Englishman at all – he looked Japanese. Only his eyes were lighter than those of most Japanese men I'd met – a sort of hazel, instead of inky brown or black.

"Who's the beautiful lady?" the strange man asked.

I snorted. Beautiful whale, maybe. Apalala kicked her agreement at my battered bladder.

"She's not just any lady. This is my beautiful wife, Maria," William replied. I met his laughing eyes and didn't protest. "Lass, this is Kent Warwick. We attended university together and when I felt the need to leave Scotland in search of adventure, he and his father persuaded some important people to have me exiled at this godforsaken place to keep me out of trouble." He helped me rise from my chair, wrapping an arm around me to support Apalala's weight.

"I should've known you'd manage to find trouble no matter where you went. Didn't you sink your ship on your way here?" Warwick laughed, but William's smile died.

"No, that was me," I said, inclining my head toward Warwick. I cast my memory back to the day I met Kaito on the *Trevessa*. "Ha… *Hajimemashite*, Warwick-san."

He looked taken aback. His return bow was unusually low. "*Hajimemashite*, Mrs McGregor. *Douzo yoroshiku onegaishimasu.*"

It was my turn to laugh. "You'll have to translate for me, I'm afraid. My Japanese is limited to a few words only. The ones William taught me."

"I only said I'm honoured to meet you. McGregor's kept mighty quiet about you – he didn't breathe a word about a wife in all his letters. If you sank his ship as you say, that's nine years of silence. And I can see why." His look of admiration was so lusty it made me uncomfortable.

I pressed closer to William. "We met on the *Trevessa*. Our lifeboats and, indeed, our lives were separated until recently." I glanced at the cove, but all three piers stood empty, their lower supports bombarded by today's swell. "How did you reach Christmas Island, Mr Warwick?"

He nodded at the ocean, lifting his chin to point at the horizon, where I could just discern a freighter drifting offshore. "The *Miharu Maru* brought me most of the way, but I got impatient waiting for your infernal cove to calm down, so some men and I took a lighter and rowed ashore." His eyes glinted. "And I'm delighted I did."

I suppressed a snort. Unless Warwick fancied whales, his misplaced compliments would land him in a lot of trouble with William. And if he did fancy whales…he'd find himself in deeper still.

"You must join us for dinner, Warwick. And afternoon tea, too, if we're not too late." William glanced at me.

I smiled and nodded. "Cook won't expect us back until the game's finished. Today she promised chocolate cakes and she knows to make extra just for you, so I'm sure there will be plenty."

Cheers erupted from the field as someone scored a goal. The boys looked exhausted. Sarah sounded the end of the match with one more whistle, sending the children home.

A red-faced Alan jogged up to Anne. "Did you see me block that goal, Mother? And that header! It almost went in. So close…"

As Anne's face lit up with a proud smile, I realised that her son was the same age as my daughter would be. Who cared for her now that Mother was here, hunting me? The only person I could think of was Wulan, my later sister's daughter and my niece, though she was twenty years my senior. The woman Mother should have chosen as her heir, instead of pursuing me.

"…isn't that right, lass?" William beamed at me.

"I'm sorry, what?"

"Warwick should walk up to the house with Mrs Jackson and Mrs Whyte," he repeated patiently.

I nodded.

Warwick looked from me to William with a confused smile on his face. "I'd much prefer to walk with Mrs McGregor."

"Mrs McGregor isn't walking up that hill in

her condition," William replied. "She has her own private chauffeur." He headed off, chuckling.

Warwick stared after him, looking even more confused than ever. Luckily, Anne, Sarah and Alan joined us then. I was spared any private conversation with Warwick as there were introductions and handshaking all around. Except for me, of course. Something about Warwick didn't ring true and I worried about what it might mean for William and I.

A throat cleared beside me. "Your ride, my lady."

I waddled in my best stately fashion to William's Triumph and mounted behind him. We set off up the slope to Rocky Point, while Apalala kicked William's back through my stomach all the way home.

Thirteen

"I cut some for you already, Mem," Cook said softly as I eyed the roast. Under my covetous gaze, she gave the pork another coat of the honey, soy and rice wine marinade that made her char siew the best I'd ever tasted. "On the table, Mem."

I dragged my gaze from dinner to the small bowl on the table. Oh, but she knew me well —

the portion of pork and sliced cucumber was just enough to fill my constrained belly. Afternoon tea seemed so long ago and dinner was an hour away. The child within me seemed to demand I eat every hour, but not enough to encroach on her space. William's daughter was far more demanding than Giuseppe's had ever been.

"What are you doing in the kitchen, lass? We need to dress for dinner and I expect you to look radiant."

I swallowed a large mouthful of pork and turned to smile at William.

He laughed. "You still have sauce on your lips. Come and let me help you wash that off."

Kiss it off, more like, I found as he guided me to the bedroom and enfolded me in his arms.

"Mm, you taste sweeter than usual, lass."

"Then you'll like dinner," I replied, pulling my dress off. I sponged down my skin, then decided a whole change of clothes was in order, from the underwear up. I only wished there was time for a leisurely soak in the bath together.

William pressed against my bare back, his hands cupping my belly. "I'm the luckiest man alive. Poor Warwick's sick with envy that I have such a wonderful wife."

Envy. That's one of the things I hadn't seen at afternoon tea.

"William, what happened to your jealousy? He stares at me more than most men, but you're not cursing his ancestors like you used to do to every man who so much as glanced in my direction." I looked down, but I couldn't even see my feet any more. A man who desired me now was either delusional or incredibly loyal like William. "Never mind."

"I've seen how Warwick looks at you, lass, but he's one of my closest friends. Warwick is a man of honour and while he might want what's mine, he'd never stoop to snatch it from me." William pulled on a fresh shirt and began buttoning it.

"You make me sound like a chocolate cake,"

I grumbled as I arched my back to fasten my brassiere.

"I'll take you over chocolate cake any day."

I pulled my dress over my head. A loan from Anne, for none of my evening dresses fitted over Apalala. Wait. Over chocolate cake? Did he mean…

"You'd get crumbs in the bed," I said, seizing a comb.

William plucked the comb from my hand. "Who said anything about the bed? The dining table is well-built and usually where we keep the cakes." He led me gently toward the bed, where we both perched on the edge so he could comb my hair.

I closed my eyes in bliss. I'd never grow tired of letting him stroke my hair into submission. Nothing calmed me quite like this. I drew a deep breath and exhaled. "Man of honour he may be, but I don't trust your friend Warwick. I sense he's hiding something."

"So do I, lass. I intend to draw it out of him tonight over whisky. He brought a bottle from

Japan that he insists is as good as the stuff from home. We'll see."

I breathed a sigh of relief as I let William work the tangles out of my hair. If only my tangled mind could be so easily calmed. Later, surely. William was a persuasive man, after all.

Fourteen

Amah cleared the dessert plates away as I struggled to conceal my frustration. Warwick had told all manner of tales about life in Japan, from the communal baths to eating with a pair of sticks while sitting on the floor, as Sarah gasped and William and I waited. Waited for him to tell something of import, but his restlessness only grew as the meal progressed.

Finally, I could stand it no longer – I'd drunk too much with dinner. Anything more than a cup inspired the baby in my belly to bounce upon my bladder as if it was some sort of perverse game. I hoped that one day, when she was grown and a mother herself, her own child would engage in similar antics during her pregnancy.

I stood, excused myself before either of the men could rise from their chairs, and hurried to the bathroom to relieve myself before Apalala forced me to do it on the floor.

When I'd seen to my body's needs, I returned to the dining room. I could already hear the men's voices, but Sarah was strangely quiet. Perhaps she'd retired to the drawing room to allow the men to drink their whisky alone?

"Where did you find such a perfect wife? She reminds me of the best geisha back home. Every movement like a dance and her appearance is nothing short of breathtaking. I'm not surprised you wanted to start a family right away with that one!" Warwick laughed loudly and slurped something.

"My wife isn't a whore, Warwick." I heard the warning tone in William's voice.

"Nor are geisha, man. They're like the courtesans of old, but every one of them is mistress of her own destiny. And none will stoop to marry a man. Beautiful enough to bewitch a man into asking, though." He sighed heavily. "None of them can hold a candle to your Helen, though."

"My wife's name is Maria, not Helen."

Warwick paused, possibly to take another drink. "Are you sure her name isn't Helen? She did say she sank that ship. Helen launched a thousand ships. Perhaps your wife is trying to emulate her in sinking that many?"

"I hope not," William replied. "Helen left her husband and started a war that rocked the ancient world. Much like the Great War here. Let's hope it's thousands of years before people start another war like it. Here, let's drink a toast to peace with your Japanese

Suntory whisky."

I heard the clink of glasses and the sound of sipping.

"I wish you were right, truly I do, but war is inevitable." Warwick gave a great sniff. "They invaded the northern part of China. Manchuria, it was called. Can't remember what the Japanese named it. And they slaughtered thousands of civilians. When the League of Nations heard, they condemned it. Outright told them they had to leave China and go home. But the Japanese don't back down. Oh no. Honour means too much to them. Instead, they walked out of the League. Every day, I received word of more forays into China. They want to conquer it all – all the resources they want and all the people, too. And they will. It's only a matter of time."

William laughed. "The League of Nations is why there won't be another war. Every other nation will stand against them. Fight them. They can't win."

"They can. The League has no power if they

can't make Japan leave China, and they're showing their weakness to the world now. It will come to war again and Japan won't stop at China. They'll take Singapore and even this place, too. All of Asia, or so I've heard."

William snorted. "You're a foreigner to them, for all your mother was Japanese. You've told me that. Why would they confide their plans in you, knowing you're an enemy?"

"They don't. Not the men, at any rate. If you want to know the state of politics in Japan, you must ask the geisha. Those who are courted by the great men in government. There are three women who are said to have their hand on the political pulse of the country. Midori and Miyako, and a third one with striking grey eyes I will never forget. Kaori, her name is. All of them looked as young as your wife, but they knew things…more than rumours. Things they'd heard from powerful men. They protected their sources, but the information…ah, the stuff of nightmares. Plans to conquer all of Asia, including this island, for the rich resources they want. Submarine ships so small they can be operated by only two men, and go unnoticed by ships on the surface."

"Just stories, man. No one can build an underwater ship that small. It would run out of air much too quickly and the men aboard would die before they could do any damage. How much whisky did you drink before your Japanese girls spun their stories?"

"Not enough. Not nearly enough. For I saw the submarine with my own eyes in Hiroshima. They were testing the prototype one day I was in the port with my father. Then when they left the League of Nations…my mother and father sold their holdings in Japan and moved to England. He promised her a house with floors and furniture just like we had in Kyoto – he even shipped half of it with them. I stayed to dispose of the last of our Japanese assets, then took ship for Singapore. When I saw the city…I knew the plans were true, too. Singapore will fall. They'll take Singapore and they'll take China, then conquer everywhere in between. Nowhere in Asia is safe. Least of all the islands of the Straits Settlements. You can't defend this place. They won't even need submarines. You have no defences here. You should leave. Take your lovely wife and baby and go far from here. Home to Scotland, perhaps. Or the Japanese will slaughter everyone here like they did Chinamen in Manchuria." Warwick gave a great gulp that sounded more like a sob and clinked his glass to the table.

Youthful-looking women who were wise beyond their years. My kind, surely. Was I not the only mermaid who lived on land? Were these women…Miyako, Midori and Kaori, all people of the ocean's gift? I knew nothing of people of the Pacific Ocean, but wherever there was warm, shallow water and protective reefs, my people would congregate. They knew as well as I did that war would affect us all.

I peeked through the dining room doorway and caught William's eye. He looked pained, as if he knew I'd heard everything. It was hard news for both of us, if it were true. But such a warning could hardly be ignored.

"Enough of serious topics for one night, eh, Warwick? Perhaps we should join the ladies. My wife lived in Australia for some time, and she has some very funny stories about incidents that happened in the fish market. Ask her to tell you the one about the escaped crabs."

I slipped away, hurrying as much as my bulk would allow me, and sank gratefully onto the sofa beside Sarah.

Her forehead creased with concern. "Are you feeling well?"

"Well enough." My heart was too heavy to tell her what I'd heard. The world didn't need another war, but it seemed we'd have one whether we wanted it or not.

Fifteen

I retired early, but William stayed awake long into the night, talking to his friend. The next morning there were dark shadows beneath his eyes at breakfast, but I knew it had been years since the two men had seen each other, so I didn't comment. William had looked equally worn out after his first night on Christmas Island with me, too, though probably for different reasons.

I squinted at his face. Was the bruising around one eye darker than the other? Surely not. It must have been a trick of the light.

Warwick went with him to work, talking animatedly about his hopes for a tour of the island, so I was spared the man's company as I took my customary seat on the veranda to read a book. Homer's *Iliad* captured my interest this morning. I'd never actually read it for myself — only listened to William's melodic voice as he read it aloud to me on the deck of the *Islander*. Only now did I realise that I'd paid little attention to the words, for I couldn't remember them. Me, with my usually faultless memory that allowed me to recall every conversation from our ill-fated voyage on the *Trevessa*.

I found tears falling unchecked as I read the archaic phrases, translated from a time more ancient than even my people's grasp of history, or so I believed. A young mother driven from her home and her daughter by misplaced passion. An absence of ten years, the same as me, while battle raged and men died, including the man she loved, before she returned to her homeland and was content.

I threw the book down in disgust. It was as bad as a fairy tale. To stand on the walls and weep while men died for her, without taking a hand to shape her own destiny? And then accepting that her ten years' absence meant nothing and returning to her life as if nothing had happened? I would not stand and weep if someone murdered the man I love. I'd take up every weapon at my disposal and go forth into battle myself – alone, if need be. And I would not go peacefully back to the life I'd left. Were all human women so weak?

If Warwick's war came to pass, was I expected to stand back and not sink ships to defend those I loved? And what about the submarine vessels – those that travelled under the surface as my people did? What danger did they hold for my people, as humans entered our world on an equal footing for the first time?

"You look worried, lass." William climbed the veranda steps wearily. My gaze darted past him, but he was alone. "Jackson took Warwick for a tour of the island. I loaned him my Triumph for the day. He's probably having lunch at South Point."

My breath hissed out in a long sigh of relief.

Once again, William seemed to be reading my mind. "Is it what he said last night about the threat of war?"

I nodded.

"It's the nature of men to want to fight. For land or wealth or freedom or even a woman." He nodded at my book. "But the world is still reeling from the Great War. Whatever plans Japan has, they won't include standing on our doorstep tomorrow. Warwick saw the first submarine – the sort engineers and shipwrights build to test, to see if their concept will work. It could be ten years or more before the design is good enough to build ships to send to war. And even if the designs are perfect now, they take time to build in sufficient numbers to mount an invasion. A lot can happen in that time."

I found my voice. "So war is inevitable?"

William chuckled, but it sounded hollow. "Even I can't say that, lass. I hope it isn't and that this is all a storm in a teacup. But I won't put our family at risk. When the *Islander* returns, I'm taking you somewhere far from here. If what Warwick says is true and Singapore isn't safe, then Fremantle is our best hope. I'll sail to the ends of the Earth to protect you, but it won't come to that."

For all his cheerful words, I heard the worry behind them and a cold cloud of dread enveloped my heart. How many ships would I have to burn to protect my family this time?

Sixteen

For the second night in a row, Warwick entertained us with tales from his past. Tonight, it was university life and William seemed to feature prominently in all of them. It was hard to imagine William as a boy who'd sneak out at night to take a girl a message, then plead that he'd gotten lost and believed her room to be his own when he'd been caught.

Or who'd drink a whole bottle of his professor's prized whisky and replace the contents with tea.

I smiled politely and picked at my food until I was startled by William's loud laughter. What joke had I missed?

"It'll be the last time, I promise you! You won't be so lucky in tonight's rematch!" William insisted.

Warwick leaned back in his chair and grinned. "Bluster and bravado, man. I'll give you a second shiner tonight, so your eyes will match. You'll look like one of those Chinese, bamboo-eating bears. What are they called? Pandas. That's it. Your own wife won't recognise you!"

So I hadn't imagined the darkening bruise around William's eye. The two men had been fighting and they meant to repeat the match tonight. Well, I wouldn't retire as early as I did last night – I'd stay in the drawing room with them until dawn if need be.

Cook strode into the room with her head

held high. I sat up straight – I recognised the signs that she'd prepared something she was particularly proud of. The golden-brown balls she carried didn't look remarkable, but I reserved judgement as she set one before me.

"You'll like this, Mem," she said softly, nudging my dessert spoon.

I thanked her and pierced the ball with my spoon, slicing off a tiny piece of cake and toasted coconut. It was sweet and crisp, but nothing unusual. I glanced at Cook, trying not to look puzzled.

"More, Mem."

I dug the spoon deeper, attempting to slice a larger piece, but I met resistance that certainly wasn't cake. Intrigued, I forced the spoon through it and lifted it to my lips. The metal was cold and I had barely an instant to register this before the dessert hit my tongue. Hot, crisp cake wrapped around…"Ice cream!" I exclaimed as I peered down at my plate. A second spoon of the cold confection slid down my throat, then a third.

"Is it good, lass?"

I glanced up to realise the others were staring at me, their balls untouched.

"It's delicious. Cook's outdone herself again," I replied with a smile for her and a heartfelt, "Thank you."

William and Sarah dipped their spoons and added their compliments to mine, but Warwick still didn't take his eyes off me.

"Your dessert will grow cold, Mr Warwick. Or warm. Either way, it will not be at its best. I assure you, it's best eaten fresh." I eyed his plate pointedly.

"Yes." He made no move to touch it. "Where did McGregor find you?"

I met his gaze squarely. "I was drifting after the loss of my first husband. It was…an unhappy place. He showed me that there was still some joy in life, if I was willing to see it. And taste it, as it turned out."

William laughed. "If you'd seen her face the day she first tasted chocolate…my God, man, you'd have fallen in love on the spot, too."

Uncomfortably aware of Warwick's continued scrutiny even as he capitulated and ate his dessert, I focussed on finishing mine. I ate too much and it was too late by the time I realised. Little Apalala drummed her tiny fists and tail flukes against my insides in angry protest.

"Shall we go to the drawing room and leave the men to their whisky?" Sarah asked, throwing her napkin on the table before rising. Her eyes were filled with concern.

I nodded and waddled out after her, but detoured to the bathroom instead. On my way back, I peeped into the dining room, only to find it empty. Perhaps they'd not bothered with whisky after all. I trudged to the drawing room, where Sarah waited, leafing through a book.

"Where are they?" I asked in alarm.

"They went for a walk, they said. Something about a wager. William said not to wait up for him." She smiled. "I agree. You don't look well today and some extra rest should do you good."

I tried to keep my face blank as I nodded and turned to head for my bedroom. I had no intention of sleeping, though. I intended to stop this fight before Warwick could harm William any more.

I pulled on my riding pants, letting them hang low on my hips because there was no way they'd stretch over my belly. I donned one of William's loose shirts to cover the rest of me and shrugged on a leather jacket, though I couldn't close it around Apalala. Her father should know better.

Luckily, my feet were not so swollen that they couldn't fit into my boots. I crammed on a hat as I tried to move soundlessly through the house. Amah and Cook were clearing the plates, so I hoped their clinking covered any noise I made.

My Triumph stood beside William's, ready to go. I didn't bother igniting the front light as my night vision was more than good enough to see the road ahead, not to mention the controls that I knew almost as well as William now. Kicking the motorcycle into life, I waited a few moments for it to reach a steady chug before I set off for the padang. Surely William and Warwick wouldn't have gone far…

But the padang was dark and empty. The only lights visible were in houses or in the port. Sibilant waves licked the beach, their muted crash the loudest sound in Flying Fish Cove. No, there was no fight here tonight. That meant…the Grotto. Where Mother waited, unpredictable and deadly.

I unleashed a spray of sand as I yanked the Triumph into a tight turn, back the way I'd come. With the throttle open full, I leaned over, pressing my belly against the fuel tank as I hunched over to coax greater speed out of it. I had to reach them before Mother harmed William.

If I didn't…I didn't even want to contemplate the consequences.

Seventeen

I turned the engine off when I hit the downhill slope, knowing I could coast to the Grotto on my Triumph just as easily as I'd done with my bicycle in Fremantle. Over the quiet crunch of my tyres rolling through the mud, I heard the crowd long before I saw them. Shouts of encouragement and disappointment melded together in a maelstrom of noise. Of course they wouldn't hear my approach.

I stood the Triumph on its stand, just out of sight of the clearing, and padded across the trampled grass to join them. Miners, all of them – Malay and Chinese, mostly, with a couple of Sikh turbans bobbing among the crowd. They pushed and shoved, waving their arms and pumping their fists so I couldn't see over the top of them to the combatants. Not that I needed to. It was William and Warwick, I was certain of it.

Shielding my belly with my arms, I shouldered my way through the crowd. Once I'd created a parting in the wave of humanity, the gap spread as men stared. So much for a secret meeting. Secret from Jackson and the other Europeans; secret from the womenfolk back at Settlement. My presence here sent all their secrecy up in smoke.

I broke through the crush of onlookers into the ring and my eyes met Warwick's. Instead of finishing the kick he was poised to deliver, he overbalanced and William's well-placed block caught him in the midsection, forcing the air out of his lungs as it sent him to land on his backside several feet away. Warwick just sat there, not rising or tearing his eyes away from me.

I wondered if there was ice cream on my chin that I'd missed. I glanced down. Ah, no. My belly had popped open some of the buttons on William's shirt, a problem I quickly rectified.

William spun clumsily on the spot. He was tired and out of breath, sweat gleaming on his body, but when his eyes widened at the sight of me, he straightened as if I'd imagined his exhaustion. "Lass, a fight is no place for a lady."

I drew myself up. "It's no place for any of you or you'd be doing this on the padang in daylight instead of meeting in the jungle in the dark."

William sighed. "It's one fight, lass. A friendly bout between Warwick and I. A lot of men have placed wagers and we must finish it, for Ong won't return their money if the match is forfeit."

Across the rough ring, Ong, the Chinese man who loved monster movies, grinned.

William extended a hand to Warwick. "Get up, man. That round doesn't count because there were more than two of us in the ring. We start again."

Warwick nodded and clambered to his feet.

"Lass, please. I don't want you to get hurt."

I scanned the crowd, but I saw no sign of another woman. That meant Mother was still in the Grotto, if she was here at all. I allowed William to guide me to the edge of the ring. The fight began again and men quickly moved in front of me, blocking my view of the combatants. I edged toward the cave, thinking to stand guard between the men and Mother.

I heard the smack of flesh on flesh, followed by William's cry of pain.

Men risked their money, knowing they could lose it all. What did it matter to me? I didn't want William hurt, either. Mother wasn't the only danger here.

"I won't let this happen!" I roared, shoving through the crowd. I shot into the ring and stumbled between the two men, just in time to see Warwick's foot headed for my face.

"NO!" William shouted, grabbing me and turning us both so Warwick's kick thumped against his side. I felt William's body jerk as he grunted in pain.

"Let me go!" I insisted, struggling in his grasp, but still he tried to shield me.

A cold, wet hand closed on my wrist.

"Human, no man touches the ocean's gift without her permission," Mother purred, fixing her imperious gaze on William. Her fingers caressed my belly, leaving a trail of damp cotton in their wake. *"Not even if she granted you the honour of siring her child."*

"Mother, this man is mine," I said through gritted teeth.

Behind me, I heard William whisper, "Mother?"

I'd spoken English. Mother hadn't

understood a word of it, but William had. And so had most of the other humans. I whirled to meet his eyes and found his gaze darting from her to me and back again. From the naked, blonde woman who looked young enough to be my sister to his dragon wife.

"Dragon," he mumbled, as if he'd read my thoughts through my eyes.

"They are a threat to our people. They must die," Mother said, her mouth curving into a smile. She started to sing the notes of a song of command.

"No," I whispered as I felt William's grip on me slacken. "NO!" His eyes grew dull as my mother enslaved his mind.

I stepped forward and grabbed Mother by her shoulders. *"I said no. These people are mine, not yours."*

"Then you do it, child."

Reluctantly, I raised my voice to sing the same melody as Mother had. That's where the similarity ended, though. My song was richer and more powerful, rolling over them as I desired them to forget all that had happened here tonight. The fight, the wagers, me and most of all, my misguided mother. I wept, knowing what I was taking from William with every note. Better me than my mother.

Eyes turned to me, somnolent yet wide open. *"Mine,"* I repeated.

"For only a moment," she scoffed, then commanded them to walk to the cliff and throw themselves over.

For all my confidence, I still felt a frisson of fear. Yet not a man moved. I dominated them completely. Including – my heart sank to see such a powerful man brought low – William.

Mother looked furious. This was the second time I'd thwarted her control over a human, but this time her fury was tainted with something that looked like lust. *"Kill them already,"* she commanded.

Lust for power, violence or both? I would give her neither.

I regarded her coldly. "I don't have to." I sang again, weaving words into the melody in our language, as I willed the men to obey my desires. "Forget. Cease fighting. Return to your homes and never speak of this night again, for you will not remember in the morning." William's words from this afternoon rang in my head. They were men and it was their nature to fight one another. Why couldn't they dispel their aggressive energies without hurting each other, like the boys playing football on the padang? I struggled not to laugh, forcing myself to think of what I needed them to do — to forget, cease fighting, return home and play football.

They marched out of the clearing, headed for Settlement.

I stuffed my fist in my mouth, but I burst out laughing anyway.

"You have allowed humans to live when they should die." Mother's disapproving voice sobered me instantly.

I sighed. "No, Mother. Just because you cannot command humans like I can, does not mean they have to die."

"You have also left it too late to swim to Cocos. You will give birth here in the Grotto, as my mother did. And I will assist you, as my father Dubhan did her, before we return home."

Wearily, I nodded, more to humour her than to agree with her plan. By the time I gave birth, I'd be in Fremantle far away, and I would sing to Sarah and William to make them forget that my child was born with a tail. I could swaddle her up in blankets like humans did and hide her fins until she could learn to control them. But Mother didn't need to know that.

I dragged my feet to my Triumph. It took me several tries to kickstart it because I couldn't seem to summon the energy necessary to stomp my foot properly. It wasn't just weariness. It was the heart-numbing despair of knowing what I'd done to William.

As I set off, I tried not to think about it, but my thoughts were full of nothing else.

I'd saved his life, but to do so, I'd enslaved

his very soul. The commanding nature of my song would wear off in a matter of hours, and William would wake with no memory of tonight's events or of my mother. Thank water for that. But the song's melody would lurk in his memory, leaving him more susceptible to my will and my song, as long as he lived.

I swore never to sing in his hearing again. William was a leader among men who deserved his freedom: my husband was no one's slave. Least of all mine.

Eighteen

Wracked by guilt, I barely slept. It didn't help that William snored the night long as if he'd drunk a whole bottle of whisky. Such was the mind-dulling effect of siren song. I finally fell into a light doze when he left for work, but my dreams were filled with images of William as one of the mindless monsters from Mr Ong's horror films. Was life truly worth living in such a state? Was this why my people killed controlled humans – to save them from a life with vacant eyes as some siren's thrall? Would William ever be the same again?

Listlessly, I slumped onto my chair at the breakfast table, barely tasting my tea as I nodded to all of Sarah's enquiries about my health. Even Apalala seemed sluggish this morning.

"Will, stop staring and sit down."

I blinked and turned to see William in the doorway. He shook himself at Sarah's admonishment and grinned.

"Now, I was just mesmerised looking at my beautiful wife. Don't you think motherhood suits her, Sarah?" Warm arms encircled my shoulders as William's hand tilted my chin up so he could kiss me. With slow passion, his tongue awoke mine and they danced together far more gracefully than any other part of my body could today. "Mm, I'm the luckiest man alive. And I've had Warwick telling me so all morning as his phosphate ship docked. I think he's fair in love with you, lass." Another kiss, too brief this time. "But he can't have you, for you're mine." William winked as he took his seat.

"What time did you boys return last night? I didn't hear you come home, yet you look more well-rested than your wife," Sarah observed, biting into a slice of toast.

William gulped his tea and set the cup down with a clunk. "You know, I don't remember. I must've had too much of Warwick's lethal Japanese whisky. I don't even remember coming to bed." His hand landed on my wrist. "I'll make it up to you tonight, lass. Warwick's dining with the District Officer and the Jacksons tonight, but I made my excuses on account of your health. We'll have a quiet family dinner together instead." His eyes glinted with desire.

I felt my cheeks flush, but that wasn't the only part of me heating up. Just the most visible. Perhaps I hadn't harmed William as much as I'd thought last night.

"And you didn't even ask me what I planned on doing tonight? Watching you and your wife make sheep's eyes at one another across the table until you drag her off to bed and make enough noise to keep the whole household awake is hardly my idea of a pleasant evening," Sarah snapped. She lifted her coffee cup and drank deeply.

William laughed. "No, I didn't. I told District Officer Males you'd be joining him and the Jacksons this evening, though you're welcome to send him your apologies and stay home with us instead. But don't expect sparkling after dinner conversation, for I'll want an early night alone with my wife."

Sarah dropped her napkin beside her plate and rose. "Mother would be ashamed of you, Will. Such coarse conversation at the breakfast table. I'm surprised your wife tolerates it." Her head held high, she headed out.

William's hand stroked my belly through my dress. "Sorry if I embarrassed you, lass. I'm just finding it harder and harder to resist you.

Every time I look at you, that glow on your face as our child grows inside you, I fall deeper in love with you every day."

"Me, too. Truly, it's fine William. I wouldn't want you any other way." Except naked in bed, and his eyes promised that he'd make it so.

Nineteen

Cook and Amah carried in dessert, the glass bowls already beading with condensation so I couldn't see their contents. Something cold, evidently.

"Leave the tray. We won't need you any more tonight," William said, waving them away.

I nodded my agreement and thanked them

for dinner.

William didn't say another word until they'd left, when he uncovered the bowls. "Ice cream, cold berries and chocolate sauce."

I half rose in my seat to see. "What sort of berries?"

He lifted one from the bowl. "Raspberries. Still frozen, too. These must be what Warwick was talking about when he said he'd brought us a gift — a shipment of frozen food he won in a wager with some Americans in Singapore. Have you ever tasted a fresh raspberry, lass?"

I frowned at the small berry between his fingers. "No. Strawberries and mulberries, yes, but the only raspberries I've seen were in the jam on Captain Hughes' table on the Islander." He popped the berry into my mouth before I could close it. "Oh that's…mm, tart but still sweet." Gone was my distrust on the Trevessa, when I'd objected to him trying to feed me chocolate. Now I'd taste anything he had to offer.

"Lass." William swallowed. "Do you really

want dessert tonight? The longer we stay here, the more I fantasise about taking you right here on the table."

My eyes met his and I toyed with the idea. I'd take William over chocolate any day.

He grabbed the bowls and dumped them back on the tray, along with some spoons, and threw a spare tablecloth over his shoulder. "I'll carry it all to the bedroom and we can have a picnic on the floor afterwards. I need...you, lass."

I nodded and rose, knowing that when I reached the bedroom, he followed just a step behind me.

I heard the tray clatter onto the nightstand as I pulled my dress off, feeling William's arms slide around me to free me from my underwear. I set to work on his buttons – I wanted, no, needed to feel his skin against mine. Our clothes puddled to the floor and the dance began anew, from my toes curling beside his to our tangled tongues. We stepped sideways toward the bed, moving to the drumbeat of both our hearts, as William drew me down beside him. Even pressed together, my belly jutted between us, no match for even William's considerable length.

He wasn't deterred, though. His fingers slipped between my thighs, caressing their way inside me. I arched my back, though the only sign was that my breasts thrust forward toward William's waiting mouth. My breasts tingled at his touch, the nerves in my nipples so aroused I'm not sure I noticed his fingers at all until I tensed around them as William enticed me to the cusp of tonight's first climax. With every stroke of his tongue, he drew cries and gasps from me, growing more urgent as my orgasm built. I unleashed a cry of joy as the waves washed over me.

When I opened my eyes, William was licking his fingers. "So sweet," he said. "Just like on our wedding night. Lass, I have to…have to taste…" He yanked at the bedclothes, wadding the linen and blankets into a small hillock on top of my pillows. After a moment, he spread the purloined tablecloth on top of the jumbled mess. "Lie back on this. Trust me, lass."

Of course I trusted him. I moved without hesitation, though not as quickly as I wished. The piled-up bedclothes let me recline much like one of the Islander's deck chairs, though far more comfortably.

Once again he dived between my thighs, his tongue licking at my insides. I moaned and he came up for air. "Who needs dessert when I have you?" His eyes sharpened as if a thought had struck him and he reached for the nightstand. I had no time to pay attention to his hands any more as his mouth returned to its ministrations.

"William…oh, William!" I peaked again and lay panting, but my magnificent man was only getting started. His eyes met mine over the curve of my belly as his fingers thrust inside me. Cold – so cold, flooding my overheated body with a seductive chill. "What…are you doing?"

"Your sweetness and the tart, frozen

raspberries you liked…I'm going to devour you." He chuckled, the vibration travelling through my body. His tongue probed deep inside me, drawing out the cold and replacing it with a wave of warmth.

"Oh, do that again. Please." My voice was so breathless with desire I barely recognised it. I didn't care. I was lost on a tide of pleasure and William was my moon, drawing me higher and higher until…

"Damn. We're out of raspberries."

I laughed, but my merriment turned to a breathless moan as William's fingers entered me once more. He didn't need frozen fruit to coax my moaning into another blissful scream. I could scarcely believe it when he kissed his way up my thigh to make me fall apart again.

"My turn, my turn!" I insisted.

"Lass, it's your turn all night, I promise."

I flashed my best, wicked smile. "To eat dessert." I glanced at his obvious arousal. "Lay it here." I patted my breasts.

William knelt beside me and did as I asked.

Hot and hard and undeniably male…my insides ignited even more as my eyes feasted on what I longed for. More than his hands or his mouth…but I could tease, too. I reached for the jug of chocolate sauce and poured it along his length. A warm trickle ran down the side, leaving a trail down my breasts to my belly. Laughing, I returned the jug to the tray and nudged the dish of ice cream. Another wicked thought came to me and I quickly popped a heaped spoon of the cold confection into my mouth, followed by another.

I turned back and kissed the tip of his manhood, feeling the heat through my lips even as the ice cream froze my tongue. Then I sucked him inside.

"Oh my God, lass, what did you…aargh!" Wordless exclamations were all he seemed capable of uttering after that as he tangled his fingers in my hair and thrust into my throat.

I sucked harder, tasting ice cream, chocolate and him. An irresistible dessert indeed. I hummed my satisfaction and reached for his balls, gently stroking as I felt him tense.

"Lass, lass," he gasped, but there was no stopping his climax, nor did I intend to. I drank down his essence, mixed with the sweet cloy of chocolate and ice cream, before I let him pop from my lips. "That was…that was…amazing. Ah, but you've made a terrible mess. I should help with that."

I glanced down. Chocolate was smeared across my chest, coating one nipple a darker brown than the other.

"Here." William shifted the dessert tray and set the washbowl on the edge of the nightstand. A soaked chunk of sea-sponge swam in the wash water. "After what you just did, it's definitely my turn again." Instead of the sponge, he seized the sauce jug, turning the streaks of chocolate into a sluggish stream across my breasts as I squealed in surprise. "And I'd like some ice cream, too." The spoon vanished into his mouth, but the sparkle in his eyes told me he had more mischief in mind.

His cold tongue lapped at my breasts, laving

the chocolate from my skin in great, sweeping strokes until all that remained were my darkened nipples.

"More ice cream, I think."

I attempted to catch my breath as William reached for the spoon, but I cried out as he tipped ice cream on one breast and then the other, crowning my nipples in creamy white. He plunged his fingers inside me as he took one nipple between his teeth, sucking and thrusting with equal power.

I closed my eyes, unable to think, to resist, to do anything but drown in sensation as he turned his attention from one nipple to the other and his thumb circled the bundle of nerves at the juncture of my thighs. A hoarse scream ripped out of my throat as I peaked, higher than ever before, hardly able to believe that the best was yet to come.

"I'll have to remember the trick with the ice cream, lass. Just watching your reaction while I…well, you see what you do to me." He gestured and even I gasped in surprise. How had he recovered so quickly? Or had I been so lost in his loving touch that time had flowed past me without me noticing?

"Yes, oh yes," I murmured, reaching for him.

He grabbed the sponge and squeezed the water from it. "Ah, first I promised to take care of the mess. And as I made it worse, I owe you that." He stroked the sponge across my belly, a strange sea-caress from my land-bound husband. Apalala squirmed and kicked it, her fluke-clad feet showing clearly through my skin for an instant before she subsided. William laughed and teased her again. She grew tired of the game before he did, perhaps frustrated by the confined space she moved in, and William turned his attention to my breasts once more. The nerves in my swollen nipples sparked at the slightest touch and though William's strokes were feather-light, it still felt like he was scrubbing me raw. When he was done, the sponge splashed back into the murky water and he grinned at me. "I know just what will soothe those." He held up two raspberries, ice crystals still clinging to them. "These were hiding under the spoons, so I missed them. Still frozen." Gently, he pressed one to my nipple, enveloping it in soothing coolness before doing the same for the other. "I might leave those there for the moment." I glanced down to see that he'd slipped them like tiny cups over my nipples, where they seemed quite secure. "Now, I believe it's your turn, if you want, lass."

"I want you," I said simply.

"Then you shall have me, lass." He reclined on the bed, his manhood extended in a mute invitation. No, a promise. With William's help, I eased into his lap, revelling in the feel of his skin on mine. Something cold tumbled to my thigh. I glanced down and caught a glimpse of glistening red.

"You're so hot, lass, you melted the ice just by touching them." He lifted the raspberry to my lips and I took it as he sucked the other off my breast. "I'm burning for you already."

Grinning, he surged into me, then out again, sweeping me away in a never-ending swell of pleasure that was ours alone.

Locked together, William and I formed a perfect union of sea and shore. We were the waves and the sand, shaping and defining as we clashed, sucked and stroked one another, parting only to rush together again in a maelstrom of passion that churned to foam on the surface. But in the depths below, our unquenchable love still swam and we rose together as one, our cries at the pinnacle of bliss mingling with the stars.

Afterward, he spooned close to me, a ridge of hard muscle along my back. All muscles but one. "I only wish we could do this all night, every night. But I worry about tiring you too much. I know you need more sleep now."

"I wish we could, too. Aren't you tired?"

"You wore me out, lass. At least, for a while." His arms tightened around me.

I sighed in contentment. "William?"
"Mm?"

"When…when you're ready for more, wake me, please. I wake every hour or two during the night anyway."

"If you're sure, lass. God, I love you."

"Mmm." I sank into sleep.

It seemed barely a moment later before I felt an insistent pressure against my back, though the risen moon shining through the window told me I'd slept for hours. "Lass?"

Not just insistent. Hot and pulsing with arousal. As was I. "Oh yes, William. Please."

He seized my hips and a lance of lava pierced me, setting my desire alight. Over and over again, stoking it into roaring flame. "Oh yes. I love you, William. Oh, William!"

Twenty

Sarah watched me slip on my shoes with a troubled expression. "If you're not feeling up to it, stay home and rest, lass. Will might worry, but you and the baby come first. It's not like you won't see him. He'll race up the hill to check on you, you wait and see."

"I'm fine, honestly," I protested. If Apalala would only stop squirming around so much and settle a little, this pregnancy would be a whole lot easier to bear. Not for the first time, I wondered if Sarah had made a mistake in calculating my due date. I wasn't sure if my daughter would have the patience to remain inside me for another two months. If that meant a shorter sentence for me as a whale, I welcomed it. I wanted to make love with William again without Apalala kicking him.

Sarah fussed around me every step of the walk to the Club, making me want to scream at her to leave me alone. I could always sing…

A high-pitched whistle shrilled across the padang. "Send him off!" someone hollered.

"The crab's not on their team, man!"

"I don't care whose team it's on! The ball's not a damn coconut and the beast tripped me deliberately!"

Laughter erupted as the robber crab was forcibly removed from the playing field before the men resumed their football game.

One of the men from the *Miharu Maru* took a shot at the goal. His kick flew straight, rising over the Malay goalkeeper's hands and soaring toward the net.

It seemed everyone held their breath.

A red crab inching its way along the goal chose that moment to dangle over the side by one claw. The ball collided with it and the crab dropped to the grass, but the ball bounced away.

A cheer rang up, followed by Warwick's shout, "That's not fair! It would have gone straight in! Spectator interference!"

The crab ambled off the field, seemingly unhurt, as an argument ensued between Warwick and the Chinese mandor acting as referee. The mandor finally lost patience and blew a blast on his whistle, stabbing a finger in the direction of the field as he pulled what looked like a yellow notebook from his pocket. Warwick subsided and stalked away.

"If the boys have to contend with the wildlife in their games, so do the men," Sarah said, nodding in satisfaction. "That robber crab punctured three footballs last week."

Anne waved from the Club balcony and we ascended the stairs to join her for tea and cakes. The cinema was set up for the showing of some film about a grand hotel, but the men who operated it hung over the balcony, watching and cheering on the football match.

"Who's winning?" Sarah asked Anne as she settled in her seat.

"Our shore team, two goals to one. Without that crab goalkeeper, we'd have been even with the ship team. Probably a good thing they sail tomorrow – or they'll all be insisting on another match in the morning." Anne sniffed. "Jackson said they started loading at dawn to make sure there'd be time for today's match. They've been looking forward to it all week and never have they loaded a phosphate ship so fast. He's going to make the matches a regular thing – ship versus shore, he says. And perhaps South Point against Settlement on the weekends, to make sure the men get enough practice."

"Whose idea was the match?" I ventured.

Anne and Sarah exchanged a glance. "Your husband, who else? My husband can suggest all manner of things and no one will listen to a word of it, but when Mr McGregor mentioned how he and his friend Mr Warwick wanted a football match, suddenly every man on the island volunteered for the team."

I breathed a sigh of relief. My song and silly solution to the fighting had been successful. And no one would ever know but me.

A cheer rang out and a mob of men surrounded William, clapping him on the back. "Three-one," announced the mandor. Even from across the padang, William caught my eye and grinned at me.

"William is hard to resist," I said softly.

Anne laughed. "A newlywed and nearly a mother. Her head's gone soft. What shall we do with her?"

Sarah shrugged. "Wait until it's time for the baby to be born. She won't be so misty-eyed about men then. She'll be cursing him for touching her, not to mention putting the baby in her belly."

They laughed together, but I bit back my smile. Me, curse William? Never. I loved the man too much for that. I couldn't wait to place Apalala in his arms and see the love in his eyes for our daughter.

Soon the *Islander* would arrive and we'd sail for Fremantle together. The time couldn't pass fast enough.

Twenty One

"…And this is your cabin, Mrs McGregor," Captain Hughes continued, throwing open the door of the cabin I'd shared with William on our honeymoon.

For two weeks I'd watched the *Islander* drift offshore, my worry growing as my time approached. At this rate, I'd have barely a fortnight in Fremantle before Apalala entered the world. But now my tension eased.

I surveyed the room, from the twin beds that William would push together the moment he arrived to the stacked trunks in the corner. Thinking of the deckchairs and how useful they might be at night, I scanned the room, trying to work out if there was space for one in here. Well, both William and I would need to open our travelling trunks, but the rest could be moved to the hold, if there was space. So two in the room and…

I blinked and began counting them. No, that couldn't be right. Only mine were here. "Where's my husband's luggage?" I blurted out.

Hughes coughed. "Mr McGregor isn't travelling on the *Islander* to Fremantle. He only booked passage for you two ladies." He managed a sickly smile. "I'm sure you'll have a much easier voyage without him."

Hughes still thought William a wifebeater, I realised, when he was nothing of the sort.

"Then you thought wrong," I snapped,

waddling along the corridor as fast as my furious legs could carry me. "I won't leave the island without William."

"Mrs McGregor, your husband said – "

"I don't care what he said to you. If he wants to try ordering me about, he can issue his orders to me. Send word to him that I refuse to travel on the *Islander* without him. Tell him he can find me at home." I swept down the gangplank, letting my face freeze into a cold mask to match the icy hand of fear closing around my heart. I couldn't leave William here with Mother around. When she learned I'd slipped through her fins, she'd vent her fury on him.

I wondered what William would say if I told him he had to come with me, because he was in mortal danger from his murderous, mermaid mother-in-law. He wouldn't believe a word of it. What man would? And so it should be. Though for a moment, I wished it could be different. Not to have to keep my true form or my people's existence a secret from my husband…ah, what a dream. A silly fantasy, only fit for fairy tales.

I huffed and puffed as I ascended the steep slope to Rocky Point, feeling as unwieldy as a whale on land and wishing I had William's hands to help me. Or even just his motorcycle. I'd see my husband soon enough – Hughes' summons would bring him home. As usual, the exertion brought on the cramping false labour pains I'd learned to ignore. I hauled my huge body up the veranda steps and paused to rest a moment on my favourite chair. Just for a moment…

"Lass, what are you doing here? Shouldn't you be on the ship with Sarah?"

I blinked my eyes open and found William smiling down at me. I stretched my sleep-stiffened limbs. I'd slipped into slumber again, a terrible habit this late in my pregnancy. "Hughes said you're not coming," I mumbled.

"No, lass, I'm not. I have to finish constructing the chute from the incline. The last of the building materials arrived today and

I want it complete before the cyclone season starts. No one else knows the plans as well as I do and some of the final details are proving tricky, as we don't want the first landslide bringing it down into the cove. As soon as it's done, I'll take the next ship to Fremantle to see you and Sarah. My sister is an experienced midwife and she'll take good care of you through the birth and help you with little Belinda when she's born."

I shook my head firmly. "I won't leave without you. Won't let the ocean part us again."

William dropped to his knees so his eyes were level with mine. "Maria."

"William."

For a long moment, he held my gaze without saying a word. If it was a battle of wills, he'd met his match in me. I wouldn't back down. Not now. His life was too important to me.

William swallowed without blinking. "I love you, lass, and my priority is to take care of you.

You and our child. You have to board the *Islander* with Sarah. It's nearly your time and heaven knows I'm no midwife, but my sister is. If I have to carry you aboard that ship, I will."

I smiled. I'd won. He couldn't carry me any more – I'd grown too round and I was certain I weighed more than he did. "Carry a bag of your clothes instead and I'll step aboard willingly."

"Lass, I can't. I have a job to do here. No one else can – "

I became aware of warmth spreading through the cushion beneath me. I struggled to my feet and saw the dark stain on the seat. For a moment, I thought I'd lost control of my bladder, but the smell was wrong. No, my waters had broken, just as Sarah said they would. A month too early. My time had come.

"William," I interrupted. "There's no time. The baby's coming now. You can summon the coolies' doctor or you can take me to your sister. But this baby won't listen to your arguments. She's coming now."

Twenty Two

As I perched on the passenger seat on the back of William's Triumph, the pain in my midsection returned, powerful enough to make me cry out. These weren't false labour pains any more – I knew them to be the real thing. The pain faded, though, enough for me to smile at William through my tears to reassure him.

He jolted the motorcycle off its kickstand and kicked the engine into life. "Hold on, lass!" he cried as we set off.

I clutched at him, but my enormous belly and the irritable child inside made it difficult for me to reach right around him like I used to. William rode slowly, careful to avoid the biggest ruts, as he turned left toward the plateau.

"Where are we going?" I gasped out as another pain took hold. Instead of squeezing him, I dug my nails into the seat beneath me.

He glanced back at me. "Waterfall. The *Islander* had to leave port when the swell came in. She's sheltering in the lee of the island, waiting for you or sunset, whichever comes first."

Waterfall. Past the Grotto and Mother. No. Please no. Let us just ride on past without her causing trouble. We had to make it safely aboard the ship.

I panted for breath when this pain eased, too breathless to voice my panic to William as we passed the Grotto. As long as he didn't stop we'd be all right. Don't stop.

My next contraction seized me in a tight grip, squeezing a shriek of pain out of my throat.

"Maria."

I opened my eyes to meet William's.

"Whatever happens, however much pain you're in, remember that I love you more than anything in the world, and I'd take it from you if I could."

I burst into tears at the love in his eyes.

And then the world went wrong.

The Triumph shuddered beneath us as it hit an obstacle neither of us saw.

William let out a wordless roar and flew away from me over the handlebars.

Without his steadying weight, the motorcycle tipped over and threw me into the mud. Pain shot through my hip as I landed hard, but it was no worse than the contractions. I dragged my trapped leg out from under the Triumph as the engine spluttered into silence.

"William?"

No answer.

I rose onto my knees, but the birth pain gripped me in its merciless fist so I was forced to drop back down to all fours. The agonised scream I heard was mine.

When it ebbed, I forced myself to my feet, scanning the road for William. He lay perhaps ten feet in front of me and the robber crab that we'd collided with. I made it to his side before I had to drop to my hands and knees for another shrieking contraction.

"William," I rasped, reaching for his face.

His ocean-blue eyes stared up at a sky he couldn't see, his head bent at an angle no live body could manage. No breath passed through his lips as I leaned over for what I knew was our final kiss. A kiss William could no longer feel. I pressed one muddy hand to his throat and the other to his breast, feeling for a pulse I knew I wouldn't find, though I wished I was wrong. The beat to my life's melody had ceased. I broke away from him, hearing my own breath darken the air with a horrible, keening cry.

He'd never look at me with love again. The mouth which had kissed me, reassured me and told me he loved me would never utter another word. Those strong arms that had plucked me from the ocean, carried me to safety, fought for me and held me through ecstasy, grief and sleep, had lost their strength forever. Arms that would never hold our daughter as he called her his lass, told her he loved her and gave her a father's first kiss. Apalala Belinda would never know her father's love or hear his voice call her his lass. And nor would I.

William, the man I loved, no longer lived.

Something warm trickled down my cheek and I wiped it away, expecting blood. Instead, I found salt tears.

Tears William had begged me never to cry for him. Not if he could no longer comfort me.

I staggered to my feet, barely noticing the

contractions any more. I would honour his memory, his last wishes. The pain in my belly was nothing to the sensation of my heart breaking. I couldn't seem to stem the flow of tears, so I sealed my tear ducts the only way I knew how. One step. Another. The cliff was so close and the water waited below.

I glanced back one last time at William, the man I'd loved more than life itself.

Goodbye. The word seized in my throat and wouldn't come out.

And I jumped.

Twenty Three

Waves patted me sympathetically as I blinked my underwater eyelids into place. Sirens couldn't cry beneath the surface. I opened my gills, letting cold water cool my blasted heart. I tore away my clothes – the last trappings of my human existence, my life on land with William, who was no more. I'd never wear the hateful things again.

A powerful contraction seized me and I screamed. The pressure was intense – I knew I'd soon have to push her body from mine. The daughter William would never know, never hold in his arms. I screamed in frustration this time, knowing I had to find a safe place in the shallows to birth her, where sharks couldn't reach us. The subsurface mouth of the Grotto yawned before me and I undulated my way in. I swam clumsily, realising that my tail flukes hadn't extended and each kick was powered by my legs and not my tail at all. Squeezing through tunnels that were barely wide enough for a pregnant mermaid, I stopped only to shriek through the pain of each contraction. They were close now – too close. I needed to push on, push through them, to reach my grandfather's cave in time. Or I'd give birth to William's daughter in the dark.

"NO!" I shouted, the sound echoing off the tunnel walls.

Cold hands fastened around mine, dragging

me through the tunnels faster than I could swim. It wasn't until my head broke the surface that I saw her face. Mother. She'd won.

Helpless with another pain, I barely felt her lift me out of the water and onto the ledge where I'd once slept. Before William was mine.

My back pressed against the wall as she shoved my knees to my chest.

"It's time to push, child. A new heir is about to be born."

"I am no child, you BITCH!" I shrieked in English, but my body pushed obediently. I panted and pushed again. Apalala would be born in the Grotto, where our little water dragon was conceived. And I resolved to fight once more. As long I had Apalala, she would never win. And raging at my mother held the grief at bay, if only for a moment.

I roared insults at my mother that she didn't understand as I laboured through the night to bring William's daughter into the world. It felt good to finally say what I thought, without worrying about the retribution she might take on those I loved. William was beyond her reach now. So I screamed and pushed and swore some more.

Until the faint light of dawn filtered into the cave and Mother laid William's beautiful daughter on my breast, over my broken heart. Her watered gold tail slapped against my belly, and little Apalala looked up at me with his ocean-blue eyes. My throat swelled with an ocean of tears for the man I'd lost, but my siren eyes couldn't cry. And a tiny tongue of flame flickered up inside me for my daughter, filling a small part of the emptiness where my heart had once been.

"Apalala Belinda McGregor, I swear that this ocean will be yours. One day you'll rule the Elder Council as my grandmother once did, but not because of my ancestry. Because you're William McGregor's daughter, and he wanted to give you the world. It's the least I can do to honour his memory."

Faintly, I heard the sound of male voices raised in consternation.

"My God, it's McGregor! He's dead!"

"Someone send word to his wife."

"We can't reach her. The *Islander* sailed last night. Mrs McGregor is gone."

Yes, I agreed silently. You'll never reach her again, for Maria McGregor is nothing but seafoam on the surface now, while Sirena swims in the depths below. Until the time comes for me to rise again.

Twenty Four

"Two fish says they'll end her exile."

"Three that they will send her back."

"Four that the Council will not see her."

"Two more that they will take her calf."

"No!"

"They took her first calf. Why not this one?"

Gossiping dolphins – I'd know the sound anywhere. You couldn't slip beneath the surface without hearing it, though not always as loud or clear as now. I did not need to open my eyes to know the pod surrounded me, and as my mind drifted from sleep into wakefulness, I realised I had no need to ask who she was.

Yet when I blinked my eyes open, I was surprised to see my tail was nowhere in sight. Instead, legs trailed through the water, between the undulating tails of a pair of dolphins who bore my weight through the waves.

This weak body that William had loved. And the reason he'd died. His daughter was all I had left – I must protect her at all costs. But not as a human.

I closed my eyes and pressed my legs together. The slither of scaled skin caressed its way down to my toes, my tail flukes extending until I was more fish than human. My heart as cold as the sea itself.

A piercing cry broke through the waves. The sound of a baby demanding her mother.

Relief flowed through me, reminding me

that I was a mammal more than a fish. "Give her to me," I commanded.

Dolphins might be terrible gossips, but they weren't stupid. Scant seconds passed before she landed in my arms.

Little Apalala Belinda latched onto my breast as if she'd been doing it for years. Her whole body rippled as she sucked, from her wispy pale hair down to her golden tail, glinting when it caught the sunlight.

"Three that they will try to take her calf, but not succeed."

"Four!"

"Hush." No one was taking her from me. "Where are you taking us?"

Silent dolphins and the swish of waves were my only answer.

"Where are you taking us?" I pushed a stronger command into my tone. If I had to ask a third time, I would sing, and they would not resist again.

"The Elder commanded us to take you to the Council at Cocos. To see you safely home, you and the calf, or she will feed us to the sharks."

Threats instead of a simple command? How…human. For the first time, I wondered why Mother did not trust the dolphins to simply do as she said. Almost as if her song lacked strength…

Perhaps it wasn't a lack of strength so much as that her song was less powerful than mine. Not just when it came to humans, but every creature in the sea. Something to remember if Mother ever threatened me or mine again.

Twenty Five

I'd regained enough strength to swim under my own power by the time I could hear the boom of surf on the reefs that marked the edge of the atolls my people called home. My body might have recovered, but my mind was a mess. William swam in and out of my thoughts, sometimes alive, and sometimes lying in the mud with those lifeless, staring eyes that reminded me of how he was gone forever. Or how little Apalala was all I had left of him. Each and every time it happened, I would tighten my hold on her, and force myself to swim on.

The dolphins had sent word ahead of our approach, so that when we reached the Council chamber, my mother was already waiting for us outside.

"Go in, go in, do not keep them waiting, child," she scolded gently, the triumphant smile on her face softening her usually sharp tone. "The longer they wait, the less sympathetic they will be. And as you must beg them to allow you back from exile, and become part of our community again, I suggest you humble yourself as much as possible. Here, hand the babe to me – you can't have her in your arms as you prostrate yourself on the seabed before them."

Prostrate? Beg? I might have changed in my time on land, but not so much that I had any intention of ever doing either of those things.

I'd done everything the Council had asked of me, twice over. There was no shame in that.

So I straightened my shoulders, wrapped my arms firmly about Apalala, and followed Mother into the Council chamber.

The coral cave had not changed since the last time I had entered it. Curving walls, supporting six coral thrones, now occupied by the Elders of each line. Nothing had changed but me. Last time, I had been mad with grief over the loss of Giuseppe. Now, my heart felt as cold and lifeless as the ocean's depths at William's death.

If they had not ordered me to conceive another child, I never would have met William, and he would still live. His death was on their heads, as much as it was on mine.

"Now, child, what have you to ask of the Council?" Mother purred.

"I have come to show the Council my child, the second baby I have conceived at their command. By our laws, that makes me a full adult among our people, twice over, and I ask that the Council acknowledge my status as such."

For a long moment, no one spoke. Then Thanh, the green-tailed woman who wore the Facilitator's crown, said, "And what Calling will you accept, as part of our community?"

Instinct almost had me bristling at the question. Mother had trained me as a healer, and until my exile, I had always expected that would be my life. Now, though…too much had happened. I would choose my own place here, not blindly accept the one Mother had assigned me.

Finally, I said, "I am a Mother, until my daughter is old enough to begin her training in a trade."

Startled whispers broke out between the Elders, and even Mother's face showed surprise. If she'd expected me to hand William's daughter over to the Carers in the creche as I'd been forced to do with Maria, she'd be sorely disappointed.

Thanh inclined her head, acknowledging my

choice without challenging it. "And where will you reside?"

My first thought was William's bungalow on Christmas Island, where we'd known such happiness, but even as I thought of it, I knew I could not live there any more. The house belonged to the Company, not William, and would likely go to the new engineer who replaced him. Besides, William would not have wanted that. He'd wanted us to go to Fremantle, where we'd be safe from the coming war. Where I had a house down by the water that I'd inherited from Aunt Merry.

"My house in Fremantle," I said.

"And where in the sea is that?" Mother asked.

I gave her a tight smile. "It's not in the sea. It's a port city to the south, a human city, where I own a house."

The other Elders seemed shocked, or at least surprised. That one of us could even consider living on land instead of the ocean had never occurred to them.

The only exception was Mother, whose triumphant smile was back. "Oh, but you're forgetting, child, that you cannot take your baby with you. She must stay beneath the surface until she's old enough to turn her tail at will. We cannot risk discovery. Here, give the child to me. I'll see her safely to the creche, so you can be on your way." She held out her arms for Apalala, just as she had for Maria, all those years ago.

My arms still ached at the memory of such emptiness. Never again.

"Then I shall string up a hammock near Pulu Beras, until Apalala is old enough to walk on land," I said. "I wouldn't trust you with a child of my heart for a trip across this chamber, let alone all the way to the creche."

A loud sob sounded outside the chamber, followed by the churn of water as someone swam away.

Every instinct I had urged me to follow the eavesdropper, to find out who had felt this meeting important enough to listen to from outside the chamber walls. But I could not leave until the Council accepted me as a full, adult member.

Mother feigned sadness. "Ah, it seems something has upset young Maria. She was so hoping to see you after this meeting, when I told her you'd be coming."

Who'd heard me say I would not surrender her sister, after Maria herself had been stolen from me.

I would find her as soon as the Council had made their decision.

The minutes ticked by inexorably, as they deliberated, then finally accepted me as one of their own.

By the time I swam out of the chamber, Maria was long gone, and I had not the faintest idea where to find her, or what I would say when I did.

Damn Mother to the darkest depths for tricking me so.

I would have to be more careful in future, or risk losing everything.

Twenty Six

I strung my seaweed hammock between two coral bombies in the underwater gardens that flourished in the gap that separated Home Island and Direction Island, and my days began to blur together. Between feeding Apalala and seeing to her needs, before settling her down to sleep, I was forced to call my food to me, for I did not have the energy to swim far. Fortunately, the fish were plentiful. I could have lived for months on the schools of juvenile reef sharks alone, though there were days I'd have given all my tail flukes for a pot of green tea, or a plate of toast made with Aunt Merry's mulberry jam. It didn't help that the scents from the human settlement on Home Island wafted across the water when the wind blew right, transporting me back to Christmas Island and William's arms, if only in my dreams.

Of course, when I woke and found I lay in the ocean's embrace, I cried bitter tears. Motherhood with Maria had not been this lonely, though I'd been shunned by most of the community then, too. Then, my fury at the unfairness of it all, and at the Council's judgement, had occupied my thoughts. But now, without William, my mind just seemed empty, drifting about like a strand of seaweed on the current, until Apalala's cries roused me to see to her needs again.

Weeks passed in this way, then months, as

my tiny daughter grew and strengthened and then finally started to swim a little on her own. Anything that moved provoked a cry of, "Fish!" from her, followed by a bubbly cloud of giggles.

It wasn't until she started to catch and eat those fish that my cloudy melancholy seemed to shift, and I caught glimpses of the sun again, though only briefly.

The first time since Apalala's birth that I felt truly awake came in a burst of moonlight, late one evening. The wind was blowing off Home Island again, carrying the scent of food and the sounds of celebration. Music, the stamp of many feet performing a Scottish jig, the like of which I hadn't seen since the *Trevessa*, with William. A twinge twisted in my heart at the memory, but it didn't hurt quite as much any more. I wanted to seek the dancers out, instead of hiding beneath the waves, like the last time there'd been such sounds on Home Island.

I wrapped Apalala's sleeping form firmly in my hammock, singing up some dolphins to stand guard over her while I was away, before I transformed. Coolness enveloped my legs as my tail slipped away, my gills already closed as I broke the surface and breathed deeply of the night air.

Lulled by the music and the laughter, I made my way through the undergrowth, steadying myself on the palm trees until I grew accustomed to walking once more. Soon, I could see flashes of red through the trees — everyone seemed to be wearing the colour of luck tonight. Like the people of the Christmas Island kampong had for the turn of the Lunar New Year.

Was it New Year already?

I almost laughed aloud, for there was no one to ask but myself. None of the ocean's gift cared about human dates or holidays, and in the close-knit human community on Home Island, I dared not reveal myself to ask such a silly question.

So I crouched behind a large pandanus, and peered through the spiky leaves instead.

What remained of the food had been set out on a couple of tables only a few yards from my hiding place, leaving space for the revellers to dance. A wind-up gramophone took pride of place on a third table that had been placed closer to the dancers.

As a child, I'd longed to be one of them, whirling and stomping my feet as I shared their joy, but now I was content to watch, apart from the crush. Without William to partner me, I'd never dance again, for to dance was to get close to another man, and after being broken twice, I wasn't sure my heart would survive a third loss.

And yet…I was not alone. While I'd been watching the dancers, a small figure had emerged from the waves and crept up the beach. A dark-haired girl who could not have been more than nine or ten years of age, as unfamiliar with walking on legs as I had been, after so long beneath the surface.

"So is it true? You love humans so much you would desert your people, your family, for them?" the girl demanded. Her eyes shimmered with tears, but she kept them in check with a firm frown.

"I did not desert my family. The Council threw me out, ordering me to live among humans until I had another child. I stayed away, not because I wanted to, but because they made me." Yet now, I wanted nothing more than to return to land, for I had no real place here any more.

"That's not what Grandmother says. She says you hate us. You hate us so much you'd rather be a human whore than accept your responsibilities here."

If I'd become a whore, sharing my body with two human men, it was only because Sephira had demanded it of me. Every time she'd sought me out in the shallows, while I nursed Apalala, she'd offered to care the child while I whored among humans again. She'd made it sound like men were little more than ambulatory penises, existing only to sheathe themselves in some willing woman for a few stolen moments before returning to the daily drudgery that was life on land.

Once or twice, I'd tried to explain to her that humans were creatures as complex as any of the ocean's gift, but she would not listen, and soon I stopped speaking to her, too.

But poor young Maria had no choice but to listen to Sephira, as she'd dripped poison in her ears every day I'd been gone.

"Your grandmother says a lot regarding things she knows very little about. She ordered me to leave, and the Council chose not to stand against her." I took a deep breath. "I might hate her, at least a little bit, for all the pain she has caused me, but she does not control me now, and the Council have agreed my exile is over, and I am free to stay. See? I'm here, aren't I?"

Not entirely willingly – I wanted to return to Fremantle more than I could say – but not if it meant losing William's daughter as I had lost her sister, this lost little girl at my side.

"She says that you're only here because of

her. The other girl you love more than me."

The first part was not entirely untrue, but the second…my heart ached for this child I'd been forced to abandon. Would she ever forgive me?

"Did she also tell you that I nursed you for months, just as I did with Apalala, for as long as they would let me before she ripped you from my arms and sent me far away?" I snapped. "I carried your name with me in my heart, every day I was away from you. Every day."

But she wasn't listening to me any more – the tables had caught her attention.

I smiled. Back on Christmas Island, the ayahs had bribed children with coconut cakes made especially for them – William's Cook had often talked about how her coconut cakes were the best, as I would see, when my child was born. I might not have access to Cook's best, but there were enough cakes on the table that no one would miss a couple…

I reached through the pandanus and

snagged two of the cakes.

"Hey, you can't do that! What if they see you?"

I laughed softly. "There was little to see, except my arms and my head. They'd see just another human, like themselves, and if they came into the jungle to search, I could be in the water in a moment, swimming for the deeps before they even knew where to look for me." If they did see me, I would have to sing, to make them forget, so that I wouldn't have to kill them for learning our secret. I held out one of the cakes to Maria. "Here, for you."

She screwed up her nose. "Ew, that's human food. I can't eat that!"

I laughed again. "Did Grandmother tell you that? Because if she did, she lied. How do you think I survived among humans so long? I had to pretend to be one of them. Live in their houses, eat their food…" I bit into the second cake, and I understood why the Christmas Island children had liked them so much. Even I'd behave myself with one of these on offer.

"It's good. You should try it."

"If Grandmother finds out, she will be angry." Yet her hand reached for the treat, longing in her eyes.

"How will she find out, if we do not tell her? It can be our secret," I said.

Maria shook her head slowly. "The dolphins will tell her. They tell her everything."

I couldn't argue with that. They were dreadful gossips at the best of times. It would not take much of a threat to turn them into her own, personal spy network.

"Then turn your back on the beach, so the dolphins cannot see. Here, I will shield you from view." I moved so that she sat in my shadow, and held the cake out again.

Her fingers were cold as they touched mine, almost hesitant as she took the cake from my hand, as though she expected me to snatch it back or punish her for going against Sephira's wishes.

For the first time, I realised that, while Sephira's actions had cost me a decade of pain and loss, this little girl might have suffered even more than I had, remaining in my mother's cruel clutches.

"Maria," I began, turning to the girl.

Only to see her dart away, her cheeks bulging with the forbidden cake, as she dived into the sea and swam away.

I could have followed her, easily overtaken her…but what then? She only knew Sephira's cold cruelty, not the love of a mother. If I wanted to forge a bond with her, the sort Sephira had denied us both, I could not force it.

Bribery might work, if I only had a source of those cakes. If Apalala were only old enough, I could take both my girls with me to Fremantle, and learn to cook all kinds of sweets for them.

That was my goal, then – to win Maria over enough to persuade her to come with us, when the time came.

Twenty Seven

The time finally came when I tired of swimming in the shallows, subsisting on a diet of lagoon fish when the open ocean beckoned. Apalala was too young yet to take to Fremantle, but there was a creche with Carers I could go to, who might take care of my baby while I went hunting in deeper waters.

If circumstances had been different, I might

have taken Maria there, when someone needed a healer. Maybe that's what Mother had done, while I'd been gone. Had her time in the creche been a respite for Maria, away from Mother? I could not remember my nursery days, and I knew each Carer was different.

I might not have used the facility as a mother, but all the ocean's gift knew where the creche was, because it was the most precious place in the ocean, where we might defend our children if we were ever attacked.

Who would have the temerity to attack the rulers of the Indian Ocean, I could not imagine, for anyone who had tried in the past had surely perished, but the creche remained inside a cave in the North Keeling Island reef, a long swim from the South Keeling atoll humans inhabited.

I found the place empty, but for a young Carer and a toddler a little older than Apalala. Both shared the same dark skin and silvery fins, so I guessed they were mother and child.

"Can I be of assistance?" the Carer asked.

"I hope so. I am…looking for a Carer who might watch over Apalala while I go on a hunting trip," I said.

The Carer's eyes lit up. "Ah, you must be Sirena, and this is Apalala. My mother has said a great deal about you, and your return from exile."

That couldn't be good. I tightened my hold on Apalala. "Yes. Well, I suppose I could take her hunting with me…"

"No, no! Helping is what I am here for! And there are so few children, there is no one for Fidda to play with. When I was in training, I heard stories from the older Carers about how the creche used to be so busy, they needed three Carers and as many trainees to keep the children in order. Now, births are so rare with all the modern dangers of going ashore, I despaired of Fidda growing up with any other children until you arrived. Please, leave her with me and I will care for your child as if she were my own. With my own." Her dark eyes pleaded with an eloquence her words could not convey.

I found myself holding Apalala out to her. "If Sephira comes, or tries to take her away…"

"She shall not have her, I swear on my life," the Carer said. She winked. "Sephira might have most of the Council cowed, or at least afraid of her, but not my mother, and not me. My mother was Sephira's Carer, you see, and to hear her tell it, Sephira was a little monster as a child. Her mother spoiled her so, that she would sit and scream if everything did not go her way, and Mother says that monster has not gone, but merely swims beneath the surface still. A spoilt brat who will do anything to get her way."

I blinked. That…summed up Mother exactly. She'd tricked the only other members of the Gold line to their deaths so that she might become the Gold Elder. She'd sent me into exile so that she might have Maria for her own. What she wanted Apalala for, I wasn't sure, but it could not be good.

"Do you know what she's after?" I asked.

The Carer laughed. "Who knows? She's hardly going to confide in me – until you returned, I was the youngest member of the community. I'm Darma, by the way."

"Pleased to meet you, Darma," I said automatically, sticking out my hand.

"What did you say?" she asked, staring at my outstretched hand.

I'd been living on land so long, human etiquette had wormed its way into my head. I'd even spoken the phrase in English. Next thing you knew, I'd be talking about the weather and offering her tea. I lowered my hand. "Sorry. It is…a human thing."

Darma cocked her head to one side, much like a bird. "I wish I knew more about human behaviour. It certainly would have made seducing one so much easier. I mean, a few minutes of grunting and thrusting and the joining's done, which isn't too bad, but my mother said…that you liked your man. That you wanted to keep him, and you might have, if he hadn't died." Darma lowered her voice.

"My mother even said that he gave you pleasure, like we do, when paired with one of our own."

I suppose it was better than Mother calling me a whore. Though Mother evidently didn't know that whores only pretended to feel pleasure at a man's touch — I had known the real thing.

In the human world, discussing such a thing was not done. But beneath the surface…there were no humans.

I closed my eyes, and dared to remember. "Giuseppe, Maria's father, loved me for days on the beach. He worshipped my body with his hands and his mouth and every other part of him for hours before we joined, and for hours afterward, too. For days after he died, I could still feel him on me, in me, like his spirit wished to worship me from beyond the grave. And the stupid thing is that he'd still be alive if I'd known more about humans — just the simple fact that they can't swim, or breathe underwater, as we can!"

Darma's voice grew breathless. "Oh, how wonderful and terrible all at once. No wonder you were so angry at the Council when you came back. If I had lost someone I loved…I can't imagine ever recovering from that."

If I had not experienced it for myself, I would not be able to imagine it, either. "I am not sure I could have recovered, if not for William. My husband, Apalala's father."

Darma's brow furrowed. "What is a husband?"

"It's like bonding, but it's what you call the human man you bond with. They called me his wife. You share a house, a bed, and it's his job to protect you, to provide for you, and your children…" William would have made a wonderful father.

"Did he worship you, too?"

Giuseppe had thought me a goddess of sorts, while William had known I was a flesh and blood woman. "No…and yes. With William, it was different. We were partners, like when two of the ocean's gift choose to bond. We gave each other equal amounts of pleasure, every night we were together. And sometimes during the day, too. He was wonderful. He made me want to stay."

"But you started swimming back as soon as you knew you were with child, of course. Because your exile was over."

I laughed softly. "I stayed with William until my birth pains began. Still sharing a bed, every night. I wish I were there still…"

But our bed would be cold without William, and there was no place for Apalala in a human cradle. She could not close her gills for another year or two yet.

"You joined with a man…when you did not need to? When you already knew you carried his child? Water…why?"

For a woman who'd known a man for little more than a few minutes of what sounded like terribly selfish sex on his part, it must be hard to imagine.

"Because…his touch made my body sing, as though I was under his spell, instead of he under the power of my song. And because I loved him. He is…was…everything I could want in a partner, or a father for my child."

"But didn't all that joining get exhausting? All that…thrusting, and other things?"

"We didn't just join. We did other things together, too. We went swimming and boating and motorcycling together. Over dinner, we talked about philosophy and leadership and…all sorts of things. He was a person. Someone to love, to spend my life with."

Her eyes were wide with wonder. "You talked to him? And used human machines? How did you learn such things?"

Aunt Merry, and William, and so many other people who helped me. "Humans taught me. It took time, and patience, and kindness and…" All things I'd grown up being told humans were incapable of, and yet…Mother had been wrong about so many things. "I can never repay them for what they did for me." Least of all Merry and William.

"Can you teach me?" she asked.

My mouth dropped open and wouldn't seem to close. Could I?

"It took years to learn what they taught me. I might not be as good a teacher, and they had books and things to help," I began.

"If you could just teach me to talk to them, it would help. I might be able to go ashore again, if I could only communicate with humans. Please, teach me. I'm willing to try, even without…what did you call them…books?"

I could not refuse the pleading look in her eyes.

"All right. When I come back from hunting," I said.

"The day after you come back, then," she said.

"And you won't let Sephira…?"

"I will keep her as close as my own daughter, and I wouldn't trust Sephira with a lock of Fidda's hair, let alone any part of her," Darma promised.

Twenty Eight

Swimming in the shallows after so long on land made me a very slow swimmer and a terrible hunter, as I soon discovered. After several fruitless hours in the deeps, I gave in and sang for my supper, summoning a wahoo close enough for me to catch.

When I was sated, I headed back to the northern atoll, my thoughts firmly fixed on those first days with Merry on the *Trevean*. I'd learned many words from William, but it was Merry who'd taught me to talk like a proper human, in sentences and such. We'd have to do it on land, too, for the words just didn't sound the same under water. Starting with words for simple things, before moving on to stringing those words together into something understandable.

By the time I arrived at the creche, I half hoped Darma would have forgotten about her desire to speak to humans. She was certainly too busy to have time for me, what with more than a dozen people milling about.

But, "There she is!" Darma said, pointing at me. Everyone turned to stare. "Sirena can speak the humans' tongue, and she promised to teach us!"

Some strange, human desire had me wanting to wet my lips, for my mouth felt terribly dry. Yet even as my tongue darted out, tasting salt, I knew I had an ocean of water to wet my lips for me. I'd hardly seen another person for months as I nursed Apalala, yet here was the largest group of ocean's gift I'd ever seen in one place.

"I've never taught before," I said.

"And we've never learned human before, but we are willing to give it a go," Darma responded, a friendly challenge in her eyes.

"We'll have to leave the water. Human speech needs lungs, and air," I said.

Darma grinned. "I know just the pool. I take Fidda there when I want to feel the wind. It's shallow enough for me to sit and still have my head out of the water, but deep enough for her to swim in it safely." She handed a sleepy Apalala to me, then took Fidda in her arms. "When these two are old enough, I want you to teach them, too."

We began with words, which they mastered quickly. The sea, the sand, the reef and what lived around us. Next, body parts, for they were the simplest to point to. They wanted more, but I was tired from my long swim, so I agreed to meet them again tomorrow. And the next day. And the day after that.

They learned to speak English, and I learned their names and histories. Some were adults like Darma and I, with children of their own, though none as young as Fidda or even Maria. The majority of my students were young women who were not yet full adults, whose fear of breeding and exile had led to many delaying their trip ashore, with their Matriarch's full agreement, though they were more than old enough to bear a child. My exile had made everyone afraid to head for land.

I discovered that Fidda, Maria and Apalala were the only real children in the entire Indian Ocean. That sent my mind into a terrible spin, for we were few enough. If we did not have children, the ocean's gift would die out.

Some days, Maria would join the class, hiding behind the others, but repeating the lesson all the same. She had not yet spoken to me again, but I hoped that day would come. Though when it did, she might be more likely to speak in English than our own tongue.

I watched, and I waited. Until she no longer came to my classes. First one day, then another, until a week had gone by without her appearing.

This did not bode well. I waited another day – still no Maria – before I went searching for answers.

Twenty Nine

As if she knew I suspected her involvement in Maria's disappearance, Sephira found me. But before I had a chance to ask about my missing daughter, she chose to reveal her reason for seeking me out.

"I hear you've been leaving your daughter alone in the creche, so that you can spread your human infatuation to the other girls. Are you planning on abandoning little Apalala like you left Maria, to set up a whorehouse onshore instead? You can go, if you wish, but you will not be taking anyone else with you. None of the Matriarchs will allow their children to succumb to your perverse human worship. It will be your body those horrible hairy humans use over and over and over again, filling you with their children that I will take away as soon as they are born, before you can corrupt them, too."

A dockside whorehouse? It would be the perfect cover for girls wishing to lay with a human, before returning to the sea. No attachments, and a ready form of income to support the girls while they were on land. I was surprised no one had thought of it before.

Then again, I would not surrender my body to just any man, even for a great deal of money.

I shook my head. Mother's mad ideas would never work, and telling her so was even more pointless. "Where is Maria?" I asked.

She narrowed her eyes. "What do you want with the girl? If you mean to take her to your new whorehouse, you are wasting your time. She is too young to breed. I forbid it."

I'd been too young to be a mother at sixteen, and Mother had not forbidden it then. Such a hypocrite.

"Where is she?" I repeated.

A sly smile crept across her face. "Even if you do find her, she will never agree to go with you. She knows you abandoned her as a baby, so that you might spend your time spreading your legs for humans instead. If I had not sent the crabs after that human you called a husband, you might be there still. Then again, once he saw Apalala, you'd have had to kill him yourself anyway, so I did you a favour there. Dead men tell no tales, or so they say."

Wait…Mother had sent the robber crab to kill William? His death hadn't been a tragic accident?

My hands tightened into fists as I imagined wrapping them around Mother's throat and throttling her. It was no less than the murderous monster deserved.

But William would not want that. He'd want me to find Maria, to protect my daughters, to take them somewhere safe, where the coming war would never touch them.

"If you are so certain about it, then tell me where she is," I said.

Mother's eyes grew wide, as if she truly believed her barb about William had missed my heart entirely. She recovered quickly, drawing herself up with all the arrogance I'd seen far too many times to care about any more. "She's at the *Emden*, learning about the human technologies that powered the ship and its weapons, so that she might better disable such things, along with Elder Shyama. She shows some skill with machinery, or so Shyama says, so I have granted my permission for the girl to train as an Artificer."

It was my turn to be surprised. Girls of the Gold line rarely became Artificers — it was a talent that tended to run in the Black line, or occasionally the Blue. Then again, if my grandfather had truly been a Black dragon, perhaps that's where Maria had inherited her interest from.

Learning to disable human ships wasn't a bad skill to have, either. If they truly were building vessels that could travel beneath the surface and endanger our home, we would need to know how to fight those, as well as surface ships like the *Emden*.

I nodded. "Thank you." I started to swim away.

"Do not worry. I have plans for Apalala's future, just as I have for Maria's. The old ways no longer serve us, and with the blood of a dragon in their veins, they will reign supreme with me, when I come into my true power."

More madness, surely, for the ocean's gift did not have a ruler, just the Council, who held their power by democratic vote, not the strength of their bloodlines.

Shaking my head, I set off for the old shipwreck.

Thirty

Though I had spent a great deal of time in the coral reefs fringing North Keeling Island, there was one section of the reef I'd studiously tried to avoid: the Emden's grave. No one else — human or ocean's gift — seemed to share my dislike of the site, for humans had sent salvage expeditions out to the ship before it slipped deeper into the water, and Artificers like

Shyama had spent much time studying it.

Of course, none of them were responsible for inciting the sea battle that had resulted in the shipwreck, with countless deaths on both sides. I…was not so innocent.

In my defence, I'd only been a child, unaware of the power of my voice, and I'd lost my sister and almost lost my mother in that battle, so I had hardly been in control of my emotions or my responses, but the fact remained that none of the humans might have died if not for me.

Today, visibility was low, with three shadows swimming around the hulking warship. They could have been sharks, but there was nothing here to attract predators, so I presumed the shadows belonged to my kind instead.

"Elder Shyama?" I called, figuring she was more likely to answer me than Maria.

"What is it?" A shadow swam up, resolving into a woman whose tail was as dark as ink. Elder Shyama of the Black line, if I had not already guessed.

"Good day, Elder. I came to find out why Maria has stopped attending my classes," I said.

"Your human language classes, you mean? I did not realise she had stopped. I cannot imagine why. Many people have remarked upon how much they have learned, and how much more confident they feel about going ashore. Even my own daughter..." Shyama trailed off. "I shall summon her. Maria!"

It took several shouts before she received a response, and then several more before Maria made an appearance.

"What is it?" the girl asked, staring sulkily at Shyama.

Shyama frowned. "Your mother wishes to know why you do not attend her human language classes. So do I."

Maria dragged her tail flukes through the sand, her downcast eyes intent on the design she seemed to be drawing.

"Maria, answer me, child! Why do you

refuse to learn something so important?"

So Mother had not told the truth, in saying the Matriarchs disapproved of my classes. Yet another in a long line of lies that shouldn't have surprised me.

Maria mumbled something, which Shyama asked her to repeat.

Maria raised her head to glare at me for a long moment before going back to her lines in the sand. "Grandmother forbade it."

"Your grandmother forbade you to attend your own mother's classes, where you could learn things to keep you safe and help you pass for human when you are old enough to surface? Surely not!"

Maria turned her glare on Shyama. "Grandmother said that she…" She shot a venomous look in my direction. "She said she was corrupting me, turning me into a human lover like her so that we will be their slaves, forced to live forever on land and never coming back to the sea, until we die!"

Shyama swore under her breath, a selection

of words I'd only heard the guards use on Christmas Island when they didn't know I could hear them. I wasn't certain of their meaning, but I knew enough to be certain they were not complimentary, by any stretch. "Water save us from that woman. If Duyong was still alive, we'd have replaced her long ago. She would have understood. Humans are advancing so fast, we must change, too, if we are to keep up." She turned to Maria. "If we are to hold our own against humans, if war ever comes to our islands, we must be ready. Now, back to your studies – I want to know how many guns the ship has, and the shell size each can fire. With no mistakes!" She shooed Maria away.

When Maria was out of earshot, Shyama lowered her voice. "I know you have but recently returned, and your daughter is still very young, but know that if you were to challenge her in the Council chamber, there are those who would support you as the Elder of the Gold line, if only to see her power lessened. Maybe not all of us, mind, for there are those who still believe you are her creature, and would not stand against her. But your classes…if she is so set against them, and yet you keep teaching…perhaps one day you will have the strength, and the support, to challenge her, and win."

Take my mother's place on the Council? The very thought made my head spin. The girl who had defied them, sitting among them? Surely not. They would never vote to replace my mother with me. My mother would most certainly vote against it, and all she'd need would be two more votes to secure her place. And she would get them, through fear or coercion or outright lies – she would stop at nothing to retain what power she had.

Already, I found myself shaking my head. "I'm sorry, I couldn't." I wanted to go to Fremantle, where I and my daughters would be safe from the coming war.

Shyama smiled sadly, as if she understood. "Not now, perhaps, but some day…at least think on it. After all, you have given us much to think about. My daughter, Kali, has attended every single one of your classes, and she truly believes she can venture on shore and pass for a human. She wishes to try her luck, to see if she can seduce a man with the skills you have taught her. Ordinarily, I would take her to the Council, so that she goes ashore at their command, but if she is wrong, and her skills are not sufficient, I would rather have her return than persist. Just the thought of her being exiled, as you were…" She shuddered.

"I wish her luck, and I hope when she returns, she is successfully carrying a child," I said. Water knew we needed more children, not to mention more of us willing to take our place in the world, even if we had to share more of the world with humans.

Shyama's smile brightened. "Thank you. If she returns victorious, I will make a proposal to the Council, that all children are required to attend your classes, for their own safety." She winked. "Of course, if you were to be one of the Elders, I am sure I could count on your vote of support. Think on it." And with that, she swam off to join Maria in the wreck.

Thirty One

Classes continued, and Maria returned. I tried not to think about the things Shyama had said, but sometimes, especially at night, her words preyed on me mercilessly. I wanted to be a good mother to Apalala and Maria, to help my people, to keep them safe. Sharing my knowledge of the human world was the one thing I had to offer, and I offered it gladly.

When language lessons palled, I conducted classes on human customs, or the peculiarities of living on land. Walking was something some of them had never done, and as for running or dancing…those things took time and training. I was surprised to see Fidda and Apalala learned to run sooner than any of the others, for they were finally old enough to join the class, too.

Apalala was ready to take ashore, I was sure of it. Her limited language skills were not unusual in a human of her age, and as long as she didn't turn her tail and betray her true nature, she could now pass as my human child. Yet still I lingered at the atoll. I had more to teach the others – while a child's blunders might be forgiven or overlooked, to pass as adult humans, they needed to be more practiced than they presently were.

I knew we needed to leave before war came to Cocos, but there was no sign of it yet. Even the humans of the islands heard no rumour of it. So I told myself I had time, and could stay a little longer. Just until one of my students was skilled enough to take over teaching the class. Kali had not yet returned to class, which worried me. Shyama would surely blame me if something bad happened to her daughter, and as her absence stretched longer, my worry turned to certainty that it had.

When word reached us of Kali's fate, I would go. I wouldn't wait, I'd just take Apalala, and Maria, if she'd come, and swim for Fremantle. Better to flee than wait to be exiled again, perhaps permanently this time, as would be the case if I was found responsible for the death of one of the ocean's gift.

"Mother, Mother! You must come quickly!"

The voice belonged not to Apalala, but to Maria, so anxious to get my attention that she had not noticed she'd called me her mother for the first time.

The class had ended, and the others had headed their own ways, leaving us alone. Even Darma had departed with Apalala and Fidda, who still needed a nap in the afternoon.

"What is the matter?" I asked, trying to keep my expression to one of concern, instead of triumph at being called Mother.

"It's Elder Shyama. She said she was going to explore a new shipwreck, but she wouldn't let me come with her. She said it was too deep, and she had to go alone. But Kali got to go, so I don't see why I couldn't…"

"Wait," I interrupted. "Kali has returned?"

Maria nodded. "She got back yesterday, when Grandmother was telling Elder Shyama about the wreck. It sounded so exciting – a ship that can go under the water, so that humans can swim like us! – but Shyama said I couldn't go. Then when she left this morning, she took Kali with her, and Grandmother went, too. I only know because I followed them. Grandmother swam so slow I lost sight of the others a few times, but she knew where they were going, so I just followed her. Until she vanished into the deep. I couldn't breathe, so I had to come up again to catch my breath, and before I could try again, I saw

Grandmother swimming back home. Only I didn't see Elder Shyama or Kali, and they were supposed to come to class. Do you think…something terrible has happened?"

Yes, I suspected it had, and, worse, that Sephira was responsible for it.

"Can you show me where they went?"

"Of course."

Thirty Two

I left Maria near the surface, as I descended to the sea floor. What had seemed little more than a shadow at first resolved into a ship that might have been the sister to the Trevessa, with its metal hull and row of funnels. What set it apart, however, was the metal spar wedged across the main hatch, and the pounding I could hear coming from underneath.

Water, were they trapped inside the ship? I could already feel the light-headedness that came with diving to such depths, a combination of pressure and the lack of oxygen, but to be trapped here, for who knew how long…

I yanked at the spar, to no avail, until a length of it broke off in my hand. Using it as a pry-bar, I levered it under the spar, until finally I felt it move. Inch by inch, I shifted it, until I'd cleared the hatch. The pounding from inside the hold, however, had ceased.

I needed my pry-bar to get the hatch open, what with all the pressure, and when I stuck my head inside, I feared what I might find. Would they both be dead?

I saw Shyama first, just drifting in the water. Then Kali darted at me, a pry-bar of her own in her hands, as though she meant to attack me.

I held up my hands in a human gesture of surrender — one I'd taught her in class. "I have come to help. Maria was worried when you weren't in class, and she brought me out here. She followed you and Sephira…"

"If you want to help, then help me get her to the surface. She lost consciousness some time ago, and if we don't get her some air soon, I fear she will die!"

Together, we pulled Shyama out of the hold, and swam for the surface. As the pressure eased, Kali took deep breaths, as if she'd never tasted anything so sweet, but Shyama's eyes stayed closed, as if she was unable to sense the change.

"We must get her inside the reef. It will be easier for her to breathe in the warm, shallow water," I said, remembering my training as a healer under my mother's tutelage.

"But is she…is she…"

Dead, she seemed to want to say, though she didn't dare.

"If she's going to recover, then letting the surface water flow over her gills as we swim her to safety, then immersing her in the lagoon, will help her more than anything," I said. "If she is beyond our help, then nothing we can do will make her condition worse, and we must bring her body back, to show the Council what has happened."

"What Sephira has done, you mean," Kali snapped. "She closed the door, and shouted through it that ships that could travel under water were a fantasy, no more, but that with our sacrifice, she would set the Council back on its proper path." She spat, not an easy task underwater. "Sephira told Mother she'd seen one of the sub marine ships you told us about, in the hold of a shipwreck, and she'd show it to us. We went into the hold, only to find it empty, before the hatch slammed shut and we could not get out."

Murder. Cold-blooded murder, just as she'd killed Zarrineh and her daughters. That had been to secure her place on the Council. But what could she possibly gain from killing the Elder of the Black line?

Another seat on the Council, I realised. For

with no other members of the Black line, the daughter of a Black dragon could claim that seat for her own. Or her chosen heir…

"She must be stopped," I said grimly, powering forward with Shyama in my arms. I thought I felt her move, just the slightest rise of her chest, before I saw telltale bubbles swirl from her gills. "Shyama's alive. She's alive! We must get her into the shelter of the reef."

"I'll help!"

From nowhere, Maria appeared, taking one of Shyama's arms as I took the other. Kali swam alongside us, as we headed for the nearest atoll.

Thirty Three

When darkness fell, I sent Maria home to Sephira, cautioning her not to say a word about Shyama, Kali, or where we'd been.

She nodded mutely, then swam off.

It took several hours before we could rouse Shyama, and even then she was very weak. I almost suggested we summon a Healer, only to realise that Sephira was the only Healer I knew, and I did not trust her not to do further harm to Shyama. The irony did not escape me that if I'd followed the path Sephira had laid out for me, then I'd be a qualified Healer by now, instead of a useless lump racking my brain for memories more than a decade old.

"Is there anything I can do to help you?" I asked her.

"You can challenge her," Shyama croaked. "Call her out in the Council. You'll have my vote."

No. A simple challenge wouldn't be enough. It would come down to a choice between her and me, and the Council knew me as little more than a rebellious exile, while she'd had their fear and respect for longer than I'd been alive.

I would need the support of at least half of the Council – two more. Two who would not be easily swayed from my side once they'd chosen it, either.

That meant I needed the most senior Elder – Facilitator Thanh.

"Do you know where I might find Elder Thanh?" I asked.

"I can take you," Kali said. "If you think it is safe for me to leave you here, Mother."

Shyama looked from Kali to me, then said, "I think you and the child you carry will be safer with Sirena than anywhere else in the Indian Ocean. Sephira fears her, wants her sent far away, and if she who fears nothing else is frightened by her own daughter, then we want Sirena on our side. The other Elders have daughters, too, and when they hear you are with child…we shall see. We shall see."

This was politics all over again – William's forte, not mine. Oh, to have him at my side to advise me. I would have given almost anything, even knowing that letting him in on the secret of our existence would cost him his life. Then again, he'd lost his life because of me, and my mother. The least I could do was to take hers in return.

Thirty Four

Thanh had strung her hammock in a cave on the outside edge of the reef. On a day like today, when the waves were small, it swayed and shimmied, but when the surf boomed with its full force, I imagined it would swirl like she was swimming in a storm tide. I grinned. I'd have to try it myself sometime, if I could find another cave. It had been far too long since I'd enjoyed a swim in a proper storm…

"To what do I owe this visit?" Thanh asked, looking from Kali to me and back again with probing eyes.

Kali opened her mouth first, but I waved her into silence. "I have come to ask you a question about our laws. Specifically, what happens to one of the ocean's gift who tries to take another's life?"

Thanh squinted at me. "An attempted murder, you mean? That is an old crime, one I have not seen in my lifetime. Though I have heard, long ago, when we first came to the Indian Ocean, there were such crimes. When there were still dragons in the world. The killer was brought before the Council, and sentenced. I can't remember if they were executed, or exiled, though. I do know that the killer was a dragon, and he'd killed more than once."

"So, if I were to see someone make an attempt on another's life…?" I asked.

"Then you would be honour bound to bring

them to the Council, and accuse them in front of the whole Council, so that they may defend themselves, and the Elders may sit in judgement, and pronounce a sentence on them, if such a thing is necessary."

"What if I were to accuse one of the Elders? Would she still sit in judgement?" I asked.

Thanh looked thoughtful. "One cannot justly judge oneself, to be sure. No, only the other Elders may judge her. But if she could not defend herself before the Council, or even if she could, the Elders still might choose to cast her out of the Council, for the Elders exist to protect all the ocean's gift in the Indian Ocean, and to take another's life for any other reason would be to forswear her oath, and we cannot have oathbreakers on the Council."

"What if her victim was a human? An innocent human, who knew nothing of us or our secrets, whose death could only lead to more questions, and perhaps even the threat of discovery by more humans?"

Thanh paled. "You...you would need a

witness, one who saw both the human's death and could swear honestly that they were innocent and killed by one of us." She shook her head. "If the only crime she has committed is to kill a human, even an innocent one, she has only to say she thought he was a risk to us and she will be justified. The Council will censure her, of course, but there will be no punishment." She sounded almost relieved. "I thought that one of our own had been killed. To lose even a single member of the ocean's gift, when we are so few…I am relieved that only a human life was lost."

"But we nearly…" Kali began.

"Quiet!" I commanded, putting the full force of a song into the word.

Kali's mouth opened, but no sound came out. Horror widened her eyes.

I glanced at Thanh, whose eyes were no less wide. Her mouth was open, too, but wordless.

Had I done this? My voice held power over even our own kind?

It was Dubhan's much-vaunted dragon

blood, I was sure of it.

I sang the notes that would release someone from my command, and saw both women relax.

Before either of them could say anything, I said, "What if lives have already been lost, because of the deliberate actions of a member of the Council, lives of our people, not just humans, and the murderer struck again today, and it is only by a quirk of luck that no more lives were lost?"

Thanh eyed me squarely. "If this is true, then you must bring the matter before the Council. For if one of us is killing our own, her life is forfeit. As is yours if you try to protect her."

"I will testify against her. She tried to kill me, my mother, and my unborn child!" Kali said.

Thanh nodded gravely. "Then the Council will convene in the morning, to hear the charges against the accused. I expect you both there to stand witness."

I would do more than stand witness. "As you command, Facilitator," I said, before I followed Kali out.

Thirty Five

I asked Darma to mind Apalala that night, for I knew I would not sleep for worrying about the meeting in the morning, and Apalala deserved better care than that.

If I accused my mother, she would lose her place on the Council. The only adult member of the Gold line remaining would be me, as everyone else was dead. Duyong, Zarrineh and her daughters…everyone but me and my mother, until Maria or Apalala came of age, and conceived a child.

I could not run away to Fremantle if I sat on the Council. No, I would have to stay here, and try to unravel the mess Mother had made. Keep teaching the members of the community who wanted to learn, and their children, for of course there would be more children. Once Kali told everyone about the human she'd taken for a lover, who'd fathered her child on one of the nights of pleasure they'd shared…I'd lose half my students right away, if only so they, too, could try their luck. Darma's quiet days in the creche were numbered.

I struggled to admit it, even to myself, but I'd already made up my mind. Faraway Fremantle was little more than a dream now, and my days of running…or swimming away, were done.

War would come, whether next week or next month or next year, but I could not run from that, either. I had a responsibility to my people, and if that meant leading them…I could not refuse. It was my duty, as much as anything else I had done in my life.

So when dawn came to my part of the atoll, I was ready. Ready to avenge William, and Zarrineh, and see that Kali and Shyama would be safe once more.

Mother had taken enough from me, from all of us. It was time to fight back, and no one would fight harder I would. Things were changing in the Indian Ocean, and we must change with them.

Thirty Six

When the Council meeting convened the next morning, I'm sure most of them were curious as to why. But when Kali entered the chamber to announce her pregnancy, as confirmed by two dolphins, they seemed to relax, congratulating her on becoming a full adult member of the community.

She waited until they were done, before she

said, "I have another matter I wish to bring before the Council."

"Proceed," said Thanh with perfect calm. She knew what was coming, though the others did not.

"I accuse Elder Sephira of trying to kill me, my mother, Elder Shyama, and my unborn child," Kali said.

I expected Sephira to speak, to deny it, but she merely raised her eyebrows and sat there, as if this was little more than entertainment.

My blood boiled.

Kali told her tale, of how Sephira had informed her mother about some interesting new human technology they should investigate, leading them to the spot where she said it was, before locking them inside the ship to die.

Only when she was done, did Sephira open her mouth. "Do you have any witnesses to support this ridiculous tale?"

"I bear witness to the truth of her words," Shyama said.

"As do I," I said, stepping forward.

I expected Mother to be shocked, or at least surprised. I did not expect her to smile.

"And what part did Sirena play in this little story?" Sephira asked.

Kali met my mother's eyes. "She found us, released us from the ship, and helped get us back to the atoll. Even though my mother was very weak, and Sirena had to carry her most of the way."

"How did Sirena know where to find you?" Sephira uncurled in her seat. "I think she followed us, and when no one was looking, she locked you in that ship. Perhaps so that she could rescue you, and convince you that I had been the one responsible, so that she'd have your support when she challenged me for my place on this Council. That is what you want, isn't it, Sirena? What you've always wanted. To wield the power of an Elder, a Matriarch, a senior member of this Council, to lead us to our destruction?"

I gritted my teeth. "I would have happily

stayed on Christmas Island, Mother, if you had not killed my husband and kidnapped me and my child against our will. You even threatened a pod of dolphins to do the work for you. Destruction is your mission, not mine."

Sephira rose to her full height. "Lies. You want my power. It's all you've ever wanted. You're a spoilt, selfish child and I accuse…"

"Silence!" I roared, putting the full force of a command into it this time. Not just a song, but the roar of a dragon, or so I imagined, for I had neither heard or seen a live dragon.

And silence rippled out around me, encompassing Kali, then the whole Council, before it spread to the ocean beyond. Only the sound of the waves dared disobey, for they were a force of nature that not even a siren song could command completely.

"I accuse Sephira of the Gold line of causing the deaths of Zarrineh and her daughters, sending them into a volcano field where they suffocated to death in those toxic fumes, so that she might claim a seat in this

Council.

"I accuse her of denying me my rights, as a member of the ocean's gift, when I first stood before this Council. I, in my youth and in my grief, refused to return to shore to bear a child to further my line, not knowing I already carried Maria within me. Even after I birthed her, obedient to your wishes, she exiled me, refusing to acknowledge me as an adult in this community, as was my right. Denying me my right to even speak in my defence. She is no Matriarch. Sephira not fit to decide the fate of a strand of seaweed, let alone one of our own.

"I accuse Sephira of the murder of my husband, William McGregor, an innocent human who knew nothing of our people and posed no danger to us. She killed him so that she might kidnap me, and my child, for her own nefarious purposes.

"I accuse her of the attempted murder of Shyama, Kali and Kali's unborn baby, in the hold of a ship so deep, even I struggled to reach it to rescue them. I believe she did it for the same reason she killed Zarrineh and her girls — power. The power to control the Council, for with no living Black Elder, I believe she meant to claim that place, too, giving her two seats on the Council, even if she only held one as regent until a suitable heir could be found."

I took a deep breath. "And I accuse her of lying, bearing false witness, sullying my reputation to rob me of my very real power, the only power she truly fears, for she has hidden it since the day I sank the *Emden* when I was but a child — a song more powerful than her own. A song that can silence sirens."

I met the eyes of each Council member in turn, lingering long enough to make sure they understood before I moved on. None of them said a word, for they could not — not until I permitted it.

Only then did I sing the song of release, allowing sound to enter the chamber again.

Of course, Sephira spoke first. "You see? She is a danger to us all. She should be exiled, or executed, before she kills us all."

I couldn't help it. I laughed.

Feeling everyone's eyes on me, I managed to control myself long enough to explain. "If I wanted any of you dead, I had only to say the word. You were all under my control. I could have ordered you to turn your tails, and close your gills until you drowned. I could have ordered you to slit each other's throats. I could have ordered you to forget, and you would have. Such is the power of my song. But I don't want any of you dead. Not even you, Mother, though it would grieve me little if you were.

"I have no need for more power. I am content with what I have. What I do wish, like I imagine you all do, is to be safe. To know my family is safe. To be confident that the Council govern us justly, fairly, for the good of all and not selfish ambition. To know that they will not sacrifice the lives of our own under any circumstances, and that when our daughters go ashore to beget daughters of their own, they will return whole and healthy, changed and strengthened, ready to take up their role as adults, mistresses of their own destiny, in an Indian Ocean that is safe for us all."

I took a deep breath. "I accuse Sephira of many crimes, crimes for which she has no defence. And though she calls for exile or even execution for even a single one of these crimes, I have a better solution. Too many lives have been lost through her actions, lives which would have been longer, lives which have not yet begun. I ask that you sentence her to a lifetime of service, to atone for what she has done. No longer a free adult in our community, she is to become as subservient as a child, subject to the ruling of her Matriarch, the punishment she forced on me. But instead of exile, she is to remain between the North and South Atolls always, unless in the company of another adult, and with the permission of her Matriarch. She is not to have contact with any human, without her Matriarch's express permission. This is what I ask of this Council, and nothing more." I bowed my head, and waited.

They began to whisper, then to murmur. I could almost discern the words, but not quite. They did not wish to be heard as they talked among themselves, and I had no desire to deny them that. I wished there was someone else who might take my mother's place as Elder, for I did not want it, but I knew I had no choice. Nor did they.

Finally, the chatter died down, and Thanh rose to her feet. "We have judged Sephira guilty of the crimes of which she is accused, the punishment for which should be death. But there has been enough death, as Sirena has rightly said, so I will offer you a choice, Sephira. You may choose a quick death, or a life of servitude. Which will you choose?"

Sephira spat, or tried to. It was a human gesture that did not work so well under water. "You're all fools. She'll lead you to ruin, and I only hope I live long enough to see it. I shall serve, until you see her for what she truly is, and come begging me to help you." She swam out of the chamber, without looking back.

Silence drifted through the chamber again, but it was not mine to break this time.

It was Shyama who spoke first. "I nominate Sirena as the new Elder of the Gold line."

"Vote, please. A show of hands," Thanh said.

Five hands went up, though some were hesitant. I didn't mind. I was not so certain this was a good idea, either. We didn't have a choice.

"Elder Sirena, do you accept your place on this Council?"

"Indeed I do, though my heart sorrows at the need for it," I said.

"Then join us, for Sephira's reign of terror is at an end," Thanh said.

That earned a round of nervous smiles, not least of all from Kali and me.

My mother's reign of terror might be over, but war was coming. And when it did, I only hoped we would be ready for it.

ABOUT THE AUTHOR

Demelza Carlton has always loved the ocean, but on her first snorkelling trip she found she was afraid of fish.

She has since swum with sea lions, sharks and sea cucumbers and stood on spray drenched cliffs over a seething sea as a seven-metre cyclonic swell surged in, shattering a shipwreck below.

Demelza now lives in Perth, Western Australia, the shark attack capital of the world.

The *Ocean's Gift* series was her first foray into fiction, followed by her suspense thriller *Nightmares* trilogy. She swears the *Mel Goes to Hell* series ambushed her on a crowded train and wouldn't leave her alone.

Want to know more? You can follow Demelza on Facebook, Twitter, YouTube or her website, Demelza Carlton's Place at:

www.demelzacarlton.com

More Books by Demelza Carlton

<u>**Colony: Holiday series**</u>

Cowboys and Aliens (#1)

Ghost (#2)

Vulcan (#3)

Cupid (#4)

Valentine(#5)

Prometheus (#6)

<u>**Colony: Aqua series**</u>

Halcyon (#1)

Poseidon (#2)

Apollo (#3)

<u>Siren of War series</u>

Ocean's Justice (#1)

Ocean's Widow (#2)

Ocean's Bride (#3)

Ocean's Rise (#4)

Ocean's War (#5)

How To Catch Crabs

<u>**Nightmares Trilogy**</u>

Nightmares of Caitlin Lockyer (#1)

Necessary Evil of Nathan Miller (#2)

Afterlife of Alana Miller (#3)

<u>**Mel Goes to Hell series**</u>

The Devil's Work (#1)

See You in Hell (#2)

Mel Goes to Hell (#3)

To Hell and Back (#4)

The Holiday From Hell (#5)

All Hell Breaks Loose (#6)

The Devil Goes to Heaven (#7)

<u>**Romance Island Resort series**</u>

Maid for the Rock Star (#1)

The Rock Star's Email Order Bride (#2)

The Rock Star's Virginity (#3)

The Rock Star and the Billionaire (#4)

The Rock Star Wants A Wife (#5)

The Rock Star's Wedding (#6)

Maid for the South Pole (#7)

<u>Romance a Medieval Fairytale series</u>

Enchant: Beauty and the Beast Retold

Dance: Cinderella Retold

Fly: Goose Girl Retold

Revel: Twelve Dancing Princesses
Retold

Silence: Little Mermaid Retold

Awaken: Sleeping Beauty Retold

Embellish: Brave Little Tailor Retold

Appease: Princess and the Pea Retold

Blow: Three Little Pigs Retold

Return: Hansel and Gretel Retold

Wish: Aladdin Retold

Melt: Snow Queen Retold

Spin: Rumpelstiltskin Retold

Kiss: Frog Prince Retold

Reflect: Snow White Retold

Roar: Goldilocks Retold

Cobble: Elves and the Shoemaker Retold

Float: Enchanted Horse Retold

Steal: Forty Thieves Retold

Call: Pied Piper Retold

Fall: Scheherazade Retold

Feather: Swan Maidens Retold

Curse: Rose Red Retold

Cross: Billy Goats Gruff Retold

Weave: Rapunzel Retold

Claim: Puss in Boots Retold

www.ingramcontent.com/pod-product-compliance
Lightning Source LLC
Chambersburg PA
CBHW070617170726
48291CB00003B/781